The Bobbsey Twins
In and Out

The Bobbsey Twins
In and Out
by Laura Lee Hope

©2011 SMK Books

Wilder Publications, LLC.
PO Box 3005
Radford VA 24143-3005

ISBN 10: 1-61720-310-6
ISBN 13: 978-1-61720-310-7

Table of Contents:

The Bobbsey Twins at Home

The Bobbsey twins were very busy that morning. They were all seated around the dining-room table, making houses and furnishing them. The houses were being made out of pasteboard shoe boxes, and had square holes cut in them for doors, and other long holes for windows, and had pasteboard chairs and tables, and bits of dress goods for carpets and rugs, and bits of tissue paper stuck up to the windows for lace curtains. Three of the houses were long and low, but Bert had placed his box on one end and divided it into five stories, and Flossie said it looked exactly like a "department" house in New York.

There were four of the twins. Now that sounds funny, doesn't it? But, you see, there were two sets. Bert and Nan, age eight, and Freddie and Flossie, age four.

Nan was a tall and slender girl, with a dark face and red cheeks. Her eyes were a deep brown and so were the curls that clustered around her head.

Bert was indeed a twin, not only because he was the same age as Nan, but because he looked so very much like her. To be sure, he looked like a boy, while she looked like a girl, but he had the same dark complexion, the same brown eyes and hair, and his voice was very much the same, only stronger.

Freddie and Flossie were just the opposite of their larger brother and sister. Each was short and stout, with a fair, round face, light-blue eyes and fluffy golden hair. Sometimes Papa Bobbsey called Flossie his little Fat Fairy, which always made her laugh. But Freddie didn't want to be called a fairy, so his papa called him the Fat Fireman, which pleased him very much, and made him rush around the house shouting: "Fire! fire! Clear the track for Number Two! Play away, boys, play away!" in a manner that seemed very lifelike. During the past year Freddie had seen two fires, and the work of the firemen had interested him deeply.

The Bobbsey family lived in the large town of Lakeport, situated at the head of Lake Metoka, a clear and beautiful sheet of water upon which the twins loved to go boating. Mr. Richard Bobbsey was a lumber merchant, with a large yard and docks on the lake shore, and a saw and planing mill close by. The house was a quarter of a mile away, on a fashionable street and had a small but nice garden around it, and a barn in the rear, in which the children loved at times to play.

"I'm going to cut out a fancy table cover for my parlor table," said Nan. "It's going to be the finest table cover that ever was."

"Nice as Aunt Emily's?" questioned Bert. "She's got a—a dandy, all worked in roses."

"This is going to be white, like the lace window curtains," replied Nan.

While Freddie and Flossie watched her with deep interest, she took a small square of tissue paper and folded it up several times. Then she cut curious-looking holes in the folded piece with a sharp pair of scissors. When the paper was unfolded once more a truly beautiful pattern appeared.

"Oh, how lubby!" screamed Flossie. "Make me one, Nan!"

"And me, too," put in Freddie. "I want a real red one," and he brought forth a bit of red pin-wheel paper he had been saving.

"Oh, Freddie, let me have the red paper for my stairs," cried Bert, who had had his eyes on the sheet for some time.

"No, I want a table cover, like Nanny. You take the white paper."

"Whoever saw white paper on a stairs—I mean white carpet," said Flossie.

"I'll give you a marble for the paper, Freddie," continued Bert.

But Freddie shook his head. "Want a table cover, nice as Aunt Em'ly," he answered. "Going to set a flower on the table too!" he added, and ran out of the room. When he came back he had a flower-pot in his hand half the size of his house, with a duster feather stuck in the dirt, for a flower.

"Well, I declare!" cried Nan, and burst out laughing. "Oh, Freddie, how will we ever set that on such a little pasteboard table?"

"Can set it there!" declared the little fellow, and before Nan could stop him the flower-pot went up and the pasteboard table came down and was mashed flat.

"Hullo! Freddie's breaking up housekeeping!" cried Bert.

"Oh, Freddie! do take the flower-pot away!" came from Flossie. "It's too big to go into the house."

Freddie looked perplexed for a moment. "Going to play garden around the house. This is a—a lilac tree!" And he set the flower-pot down close to Bert's elbow. Bert was now busy trying to put a pasteboard chimney on his house, and did not notice. A moment later Bert's elbow hit the flower-pot and down it went on the floor, breaking into several pieces and scattering the dirt over the rug.

"Oh, Bert! what have you done?" cried Nan, in alarm. "Get the broom and the dust-pan, before Dinah comes."

"It was Freddie's fault."

"Oh, my lilac tree is all gone!" cried the little boy. "And the boiler to my fire engine, too," he added, referring to the flower-pot, which he had used the day before when playing fireman.

At that moment, Dinah, the cook, came in from the kitchen.

"Well, I declar' to gracious!" she exclaimed. "If yo' chillun ain't gone an' mussed up de floah ag'in!"

"Bert broke my boiler!" said Freddie, and began to cry.

"Oh, never mind, Freddie, there are plenty of others in the cellar," declared Nan. "It was an accident, Dinah," she added, to the cook.

"Eberyt'ing in dis house wot happens is an accident," grumbled the cook, and went off to get the dust-pan and broom. As soon as the muss had been cleared away Nan cut out the red table cover for Freddie, which made him forget the loss of the "lilac tree" and the "boiler."

"Let us make a row of houses," suggested Flossie. "Bert's big house can be at the head of the street." And this suggestion was carried out. Fortunately, more pasteboard boxes were to be had, and from these they made shade trees and some benches, and Bert cut out a pasteboard horse and cart. To be sure, the horse did not look very lifelike, but they all played it was a horse and that was enough. When the work was complete they called Dinah in to admire it, which she did standing near the doorway with her fat hands resting on her hips.

"I do declar', it looks most tremend'us real," said the cook. "It's a wonder to me yo' chillun can make sech t'ings."

"We learned it in the kindergarten class at school," answered Nan.

"Yes, in the kindergarten," put in Flossie.

"But we don't make fire engines there," came from Freddie.

At this Dinah began to laugh, shaking from head to foot.

"Fire enjuns, am it, Freddie? Reckon yo' is gwine to be a fireman when yo' is a man, hey?"

"Yes, I'm going to be a real fireman," was the ready answer.

"An' what am yo' gwine to be, Master Bert?"

"Oh, I'm going to be a soldier," said Bert.

"I want to be a soldier, too," put in Freddie. "A soldier and a fireman."

"Oh, dear, I shouldn't want to be a soldier and kill folks," said Nan.

"Girls can't be soldiers," answered Freddie. "They have to get married, or be dressmakers, or sten'graphers, or something like that."

"You mean stenographers, Bert. I'm going to be a sten_o_grapher when I get big."

"I don't want to be any stenogerer," put in Flossie. "I'm going to keep a candy store, and have all the candy I want, and ice cream—"

"Me too!" burst in Freddie. "I'm going to have a candy store, an' be a fireman, an' a soldier, all together!"

"Dear! dear!" laughed Dinah. "Jess to heah dat now! It's wonderful wot yo' is gwine to be when yo' is big."

At that moment the front door bell rang, and all rushed to the hallway, to greet their mother, who had been down-town, on a shopping tour.

Rope Jumping, and What Followed

"Oh, mamma, what have you brought?" Such was the cry from all of the Bobbsey twins, as they gathered around Mrs. Bobbsey in the hallway. She had several small packages in her hands, and one looked very much like a box of candy.

Mrs. Bobbsey kissed them all before speaking. "Have you been good while I was gone?" she asked.

"I guess we tried to be good," answered Bert meekly.

"Freddie's boiler got broke, that's all," said Flossie. "Dinah swept up the dirt."

Before anything more could be said all were in the dining room and Mrs. Bobbsey was called upon to admire the row of houses. Then the box of candy was opened and each received a share.

"Now you had better go out and play," said the mother. "Dinah must set the table for dinner. But be sure and put on your thick coats. It is very cold and feels like snow."

"Oh, if only it would snow!" said Bert. He was anxious to try a sled he had received the Christmas before.

It was Saturday, with no school, so all of the boys and girls of the neighborhood were out. Some of the girls were skipping rope, and Nan joined these, while Bert went off to join a crowd of boys in a game of football.

"Let us play horse," suggested Freddie to Flossie. They had reins of red leather, with bells, and Freddie was the horse while his twin sister was the driver.

"I'm a bad horse, I'll run away if you don't watch me," cautioned Freddie, and began to prance around wildly, against the grape arbor and then up against the side fence.

"Whoa! whoa!" screamed Flossie, jerking on the reins. "Whoa, you naughty horse! If I had a whip, I'd beat you!"

"If you did that, I'd kick," answered Freddie, and began to kick real hard into the air. But at last he settled down and ran around the house just as nicely as any horse could. Then he snorted and ran up to the water bucket near the barn and Flossie pretended to give him a drink and some hay, and unharnessed him just as if he was a real steed.

Nan was counting while another girl named Grace Lavine jumped, Grace was a great jumper and had already passed forty when her mother called to her from the window.

"Grace, don't jump so much. You'll get sick."

"Oh, no, I won't," returned Grace. She was a headstrong girl and always wanted her own way.

"But jumping gave you a headache only last week," continued Mrs. Lavine. "Now, don't do too much of it," and then the lady closed the window and went back to her interrupted work.

"Oh, dear, mamma made me trip," sighed Grace. "I don't think that was fair."

"But your mamma doesn't want you to jump any more," put in another girl, Nellie Parks by name.

"Oh, she didn't say that. She said not to jump too much."

It was now Nan's turn to jump and she went up to twenty-seven and then tripped. Nellie followed and reached thirty-five. Then came another girl who jumped to fifty-six.

"I'm going a hundred this time," said Grace, as she skipped into place.

"Oh, Grace, you had better not!" cried Nan.

"You're afraid I'll beat you," declared Grace.

"No, I'm not. But your mamma said—"

"I don't care what she said. She didn't forbid my jumping," cut in the obstinate girl. "Are you going to turn or not?"

"Yes, I'll turn," replied Nan, and at once the jumping started. Soon Grace had reached forty. Then came fifty, and then sixty.

"I do believe she will reach a hundred after all," declared Nellie Parks, a little enviously.

"I will, if you turn steadily," answered Grace, in a panting voice. Her face was strangely pale.

"Oh, Grace, hadn't you better stop?" questioned Nan. She was a little frightened, but, nevertheless, kept on turning the rope.

"No!" puffed Grace. "Go—go on!"

She had now reached eighty-five. Nellie Parks was counting:

"Eighty-six, eighty-seven, eighty-eight, eighty-nine, ninety!" she went on. "Ninety-one-, ninety-two—"

"No—not so—so fast!" panted Grace. "I—I—oh!"

And then, just as Nellie was counting "Ninety-seven," she sank down in a heap, with her eyes closed and her face as white as a sheet.

For a moment the other girls looked on in blank wonder, not knowing what to make of it. Then Nan gave a scream.

"Oh, girls, she has fainted!"

"Perhaps she is dead!" burst out Nellie Parks. "And if she is, we killed her, for we turned the rope!"

"Oh, Nellie, please don't say that!" said Nan. She could scarcely speak the words.

"Shall I go and tell Mrs. Lavine?" asked another girl who stood near.

"No—yes," answered Nan. She was so bewildered she scarcely knew what to say. "Oh, isn't it awful!"

They gathered close around the fallen girl, but nobody dared to touch her. While they were there, and one had gone to tell Mrs. Lavine, a gentleman came up. It was Mr. Bobbsey, coming home from the lumber yard for lunch.

"What is the trouble?" he asked, and then saw Grace. "What happened to her?"

"She was—was jumping rope, and couldn't jump any more," sobbed Nan. "Oh, papa, she—isn't de—dead, is she?"

Mr. Bobbsey was startled and with good reason, for he had heard of more than one little girl dying from too much jumping. He took the limp form up in his arms and hurried to the Lavine house with it. "Run and tell Doctor Briskett," he called back to Nan.

The physician mentioned lived but a short block away, and Nan ran as fast as her feet could carry her. The doctor had just come in from making his morning calls and had his hat and overcoat still on.

"Oh, Doctor Briskett, do come at once!" she sobbed. "Grace Lavine is dead, and we did it, turning the rope for her!"

"Grace Lavine dead?" repeated the dumfounded doctor.

"Yes! yes!"

"Where is she?"

"Papa just carried her into her house."

Without waiting to hear more, Doctor Briskett ran toward the Lavine residence, around which quite a crowd had now collected. In the crowd was Bert.

"Is Grace really dead?" he asked.

"I—I—guess so," answered Nan. "Oh, Bert, it's dreadful! I was turning the rope and she had reached ninety-seven, when all at once she sank down, and—" Nan could not go on, but leaned on her twin brother's arm for support.

"You girls are crazy to jump rope so much," put in a big boy, Danny Rugg by name. Danny was something of a bully and very few of the girls liked him.

"It's no worse than playing football," said a big girl.

"Yes, it is, much worse," retorted Danny. "Rope jumping brings on heart disease. I heard father tell about it."

"I hope Grace didn't get heart disease," sobbed Nan.

"You turned the rope," went on Danny maliciously. "If she dies, they'll put you in prison, Nan Bobbsey."

"They shan't do it!" cried Bert, coming to his sister's rescue. "I won't let them."

"Much you can stop 'em, Bert Bobbsey."

"Can't I?"

"No, you can't."

"I'll see if I can't," answered Bert, and he gave Danny such a look that the latter edged away, thinking he was going to be attacked.

Doctor Briskett had gone into the house and the crowd hung around impatiently, waiting for news. The excitement increased, and Mrs. Bobbsey came forth, followed by Freddie and Flossie, who had just finished playing horse.

"Nan, Nan! what can it mean?" said Mrs. Bobbsey.

"Oh, mamma!" murmured Nan, and sank, limp and helpless, into her mother's arms.

Just then Mr. Bobbsey came forth from the Lavine residence. Seeing his wife supporting their daughter, he hurried in that direction.

"Grace is not dead," he announced. "She had a fainting spell, that is all. But I think after this she had better leave rope skipping alone."

The First Snow Storm

Nan felt greatly relieved to learn that Grace was not dead.

"Oh, mamma, I am *so* glad!" she said, over and over again.

"I am glad too," answered Mrs. Bobbsey. "Her mamma has told her several times not to jump so much."

"Yes, I heard her." Nan's eyes dropped. "I was wicked to turn the rope for her."

In the end Nan told her mother the whole story, to which Mrs. Bobbsey listened very gravely.

"It was certainly wrong, Nan," she said. "After this I hope my little girl will try to do better."

"I shall try," answered Nan.

It was long after the dinner hour before the excitement died away. Then it was learned that Grace was resting quietly in an easy chair and the doctor had ordered that she be kept quiet for several days. She was very much frightened and had told her parents that she would never jump rope again.

The time was the fall of the year, and that Saturday evening there was a feeling of snow in the air stronger than before.

"Oh, if only it would snow!" came from Bert, several times. "I like winter better than anything."

"I don't," answered Nan. "Think of the nice flowers we have in the summer."

"You can't have much fun with flowers, Nan."

"Yes, you can. And think of the birds—"

"I like the summer," piped in Freddie, "cos then we go to the country where the cows and the chickens are!"

"Yes, and gather the eggs," put in Flossie, who had gathered eggs many times during the summer just past, while on a visit to their Uncle Daniel Bobbsey's farm at Meadow Brook. All of the Bobbsey children thought Meadow Brook the finest country place in all the world.

Bert's wish for snow was soon gratified. Sunday morning found it snowing steadily, the soft flakes coming down silently and covering the ground to the depth of several inches.

"Winter has come after all!" cried the boy. "Wish it was Monday instead of Sunday."

"The snow is not quite deep enough for sleighing yet," returned his father.

Despite the storm, all attended church in the morning, and the four children and Mrs. Bobbsey went to Sunday school in the afternoon. The lady taught a class of little girls and had Flossie as one of her pupils.

To the children, traveling back and forth through the snow was great sport, and Bert couldn't resist the temptation to make several snowballs and throw them at the other boys. The other boys threw back in return and Bert's hat was knocked off.

"Bert, this will not do on Sunday," said Mrs. Bobbsey, and there the snowballing came to an end.

All through that night the snow continued to come down, and on Monday morning it was over a foot deep. The air was crisp and cold and all of the children felt in the best of spirits.

"Nan and Bert can go to school," said Mrs. Bobbsey. "But I think Freddie and Flossie had better stay home. Walking would come too hard on them."

"I want to go out in the snow!" cried Freddie. "I don't want to stay indoors all day."

"You shall go out later on, in the garden," replied his mother.

"They can watch Sam shovel off the snow," put in Mr. Bobbsey. Sam was the man of all work. He and Dinah, the cook, were married and lived in some pleasant rooms over the stable.

"Yes, let us watch him!" cried Flossie, and soon she and Freddie were at the window, watching the colored man as he banked up the snow on either side of the garden walk and the sidewalk. Once Sam made a motion as if to throw a shovelful of snow at the window, and this made them dodge back in alarm and then laugh heartily.

The school was only a few blocks away from the Bobbsey home, but Nan and Bert had all they could do to reach it, for the wind had made the snow drift, so that in some spots it was very deep.

"Better look out or we'll get in over our heads," cried Bert.

"Oh, Bert, wouldn't it be terrible to have such a thing happen!" answered his twin sister. "How would we ever get out?"

"Ring the alarm and have the street-cleaning men dig us out," he said merrily. "Do you know, Nan, that I just love the snow. It makes me feel like singing and whistling." And he broke into a merry whistle.

"I love it because it looks so white and pure, Bert."

They were speedily joined by a number of other boys and girls, all bound for school. Some of the girls were having fun washing each other's faces and it was not long before Nan had her face washed too. The cold snow on her cheek and ear did not feel very nice, but she took the fun in good part and went to washing like the rest.

The boys were already snowballing each other, some on one side of the street and some on the other. The snowballs were flying in all directions and Bert was hit on the back and on the shoulder.

"I'll pay you back!" he cried, to Charley Mason, who had hit him in the back, and he let fly a snowball which landed directly on Charley's neck. Some of the snow went down Charley's back and made him shiver from the cold.

"I wouldn't stand that, Charley," said Danny Rugg, who was close at hand. "I'd pitch into him if I were you."

"You pitch into him," grumbled Charley. "You can throw awfully straight."

Danny prided himself on his throwing, which, however, was no better than the throwing of the other lads, and he quickly made two hard snowballs. With these in hand he ran out into the street and waited until Bert's hands were empty. Then he came up still closer and threw one of the snowballs with all his might. It struck Bert in the back of the head and sent him staggering.

"Hi! how do you like that?" roared Danny, in high glee. "Have another?" And as Bert stood up and looked around he let drive again, this time hitting Bert directly in the ear. The snowball was so hard it made Bert cry out in pain.

"For shame, Danny Rugg, to hit Bert so hard as that!" cried Nan.

"Oh, you keep still, Nan Bobbsey!" retorted Danny. "This is our sport, not yours."

"But you shouldn't have come so close before you threw the snowball."

"I know what I'm doing," growled the big boy, running off.

The whack in the ear made that member ache, and Bert did not feel near so full of fun when he entered the schoolyard. Several of his friends came up to him in sympathy.

"Did he hurt you very much, Bert?" asked one.

"He hurt me enough. It wasn't fair to come so close, or to make the snowballs so hard."

"Let us duck Danny in the snow," suggested one of the boys.

This was considered a good plan, but nobody wanted to start in, for, as I have said before, Danny was a good deal of a bully, and could get very rough at times.

While the boys were talking the matter over, the school bell rang and all had to go to their classrooms. In a little while Bert's ear stopped aching, but he did not forget how Danny Rugg had treated him.

"I'll pay him back when we go home to dinner," Bert told himself, and laid his plans accordingly.

As soon as Bert got out of school he hurried into a corner of the yard and made three good, hard snowballs. These he concealed under his overcoat and then waited for Danny to appear.

The big boy must have known that Bert would try to square matters with him, for as soon as he came out he ran in the direction of one of the main streets of Lakeport, just the opposite direction to that which he usually pursued.

"You shan't get away from me!" cried Bert, and ran after him. Soon he threw one snowball and this landed on Danny's back. Then he threw another and knocked off the bully's cap.

"Hi! stop that!" roared Danny, and stooped to pick up the cap. Whiz! came the third snowball and hit Danny on the cheek. He let out a cry of pain.

"I'll fix you for that, Bert Bobbsey!" he said, stooping down in the street. "How do you like that?"

He had picked up a large chunk of ice lying in the gutter, and now he threw it at Bert's head with all force. Bert dodged, and the ice went sailing past him and hit the show window of a small shoe store, shattering a pane of glass into a hundred pieces.

The Broken Window

Neither Danny nor Bert had expected such an ending to the snowball fight and for the moment neither knew what to do. Then, as the owner of the shoe store came running out, both set off on a run.

"Stop! stop!" roared the shoe dealer, coming after them. "Stop, I say!"

But the more he cried stop the harder they ran. Both soon reached the corner, and while Danny went up the side street, Bert went down, so the boys soon became widely separated.

Reaching the corner, the owner of the store did not know which boy to go after, but made up his mind to follow Bert, who could not run as fast as Danny. So after Bert he came, with such long steps that he was soon close to the lad.

Bert was greatly scared, for he was afraid that if he was caught he might be arrested. Seeing an alleyway close at hand, he ran into this. At the back was a fence, and with all speed he climbed up and let himself down on the other side. Then he ran around a corner of a barn, through another alleyway, and into a street leading home.

The shoe dealer might have followed, but he suddenly remembered that he had left the store unprotected and that somebody might come in and run off with his stock and his money. So he went back in a hurry; and the chase came to an end.

When Bert got home he was all out of breath, and his legs trembled so he could scarcely stand. Nan had just arrived and the family were preparing to sit down to lunch.

"Why, Bert, why do you run so hard?" protested his mother. "You must not do it. If you breathe in so much cold air, you may take cold."

"Oh, I—I'm all right," he panted, and started to drop into his seat, but Mrs. Bobbsey made him go up to the bathroom and wash up and comb his hair.

Poor Bert was in a fever of anxiety all through the meal. Every instant he expected to hear the front door bell ring, and find there a policeman to take him to the station house. He could scarcely eat a mouthful.

"What's the matter? Do you feel sick?" asked the father.

"No, I'm not sick," he answered.

"You play altogether too hard. Take it easy. The snow will last a long time," went on Mr. Bobbsey.

After lunch Bert did not dare to go back to school. But he could think of no excuse for staying home and at last set off in company with Nan. He looked around for Danny, but the big lad did not show himself.

"What's the matter with you, Bert?" questioned his twin sister, as they trudged along.

"Nothing is the matter, Nan."

"But there is. You act so strange."

"I—I don't feel very good."

"Then you did run too hard, after all."

"It wasn't that, Nan." Bert looked around him. "Do you see anything of Danny Rugg?"

"No." Nan stopped short. "Bert Bobbsey, did you have a fight with him?"

"No—that is, not a real fight. I chased him with some snowballs and he threw a big chunk of ice at me."

"Did he hit you?"

"No, he—he—oh, Nan, perhaps I had better tell you. But you must promise not to tell anybody else."

"Tell me what?"

"Will you promise not to tell?"

"Yes," said Nan promptly, for she and her twin brother always trusted each other.

"When Danny threw the ice at me it flew past and broke Mr. Ringley's window."

"What, of the shoe store?"

"Yes. Mr. Ringley came running out after both of us. I ran one way and Danny ran another. I ran into the alleyway past Jackson's barn, and got over the fence, and he didn't come any further."

"Does Mr. Ringley think you broke the window?"

"I guess he does. Anyway, he followed me and not Danny."

"But you had nothing to do with it. Oh, Bert, what made you run away at all. Why didn't you stop and tell the truth?"

"I—I got scared, that's why. I was afraid he'd get a policeman."

"Danny ought to own up that he did it."

"He won't do it. He'll put it off on me if he can,—because I chased him in the first place."

"Did Mr. Ringley know it was you?"

"I don't know. Now, Nan, remember, you promised not to tell."

"All right, Bert, I won't say a word. But—but—what do you think Mr. Ringley will do?"

"I don't know."

When they reached the school Danny Rugg was nowhere to be seen. The boys continued to have fun snowballing, but Bert had no heart for play and went to his classroom immediately. But he could not put his mind on his lessons and missed both in geography and arithmetic.

"Bert, you are not paying attention," said the teacher severely. "You just said the capital of Pennsylvania was Albany. You must know better than that."

"Philadelphia," corrected Bert.

"After this pay more attention."

Danny Rugg did not come to school, nor did he show himself until an hour after school was out. Bert had gone home and brought forth his sled, and he and Nan were giving Freddie and Flossie a ride around the block when Danny hailed Bert.

"Come here, I want to talk to you," he said, from across the street.

"What do you want?" asked Bert roughly.

"I've got something to tell you. It won't take but a minute."

Bert hesitated, and then leaving Nan to go on alone with the sled, he crossed to where Danny was standing, partly sheltered by a tree box.

"You can't blame that broken window off on me, Danny Rugg," he began.

"Hush!" whispered Danny, in alarm. "I ain't going to blame it off on you, Bert. I only want you to promise to keep quiet about it."

"Why should I? It was your fault."

"Was it? I don't think so. You began the fight. Besides, if you dare to say a word, I'll—I'll give you a big thrashing!" blustered Danny.

He clenched his fists as he spoke and looked so fierce that Bert retreated a step.

"I haven't said anything, Danny."

"Then you had better not. Old Ringley doesn't know who broke his window. So you keep quiet; do you hear?"

"Are you sure he doesn't know?"

"Yes, because he has been asking everybody about it."

There was a pause and the two boys looked at each other.

"You ought to pay for the window," said Bert.

"Huh! I'm not going to do it. You can pay for it if you want to. But don't you dare to say anything about me! If you do, you'll catch it, I can tell you!" And then Danny walked off.

"What did he have to say?" questioned Nan, when Bert came back to her.

"He wants me to keep still. He says Mr. Ringley doesn't know who did it."

"Did you promise to keep still, Bert?"

"No, but if I say anything Danny says he will give it to me."

A crowd of boys and girls now came up and the talk was changed. All were having a merry time in the snow, and for the time being Bert forgot his troubles. He and Nan gave Freddie and Flossie a long ride which pleased the younger twins very much.

"I wish you was really and truly horses," said Flossie. "You go so *beau*tifully!"

"And if I had a whip I could make you go faster," put in Freddie.

"For shame, Freddie!" exclaimed Nan. "Would you hit the horse that gave you such a nice ride?"

"Let me give *you* a ride," answered the little fellow, to change the subject.

He insisted upon it, and soon Nan was on the sled behind Flossie, and Bert and Freddie were hauling them along where pulling was easy. This was great sport for Freddie, and he puffed and snorted like a real horse, and kicked up his heels, very much to Flossie's delight.

"Gee-dap!" shrieked the little maiden. "Gee-dap!" and moved back and forth on the sled, to make it go faster. Away went Freddie and Bert, as fast as the legs of the little fellow could travel. They went down a long hill and through a nice side street, and it was a good half hour before they reached home,—just in time for a good hot supper.

Bert's Ghost

Bert felt relieved to learn that Mr. Ringley did not know who had broken the store window, but he was still fearful that the offense might be laid at his door. He was afraid to trust Danny Rugg, and did not know what the big boy might do.

"He may say I did it, just to clear himself," thought Bert. "And if Mr. Ringley comes after me, he'll remember me sure."

But his anxiety was forgotten that evening, when some of the neighbors dropped in for a call. There was music on the piano and some singing, and almost before Bert and Nan knew it, it was time to go to bed. Freddie and Flossie had already retired, worn out by their play.

But after Bert had said his prayers and found himself alone in the small bed chamber he occupied, he could not sleep. The talk of the folks below kept him awake at first, and even after they had gone to bed he could not forget the happening of the day, and he could still hear the crash of that glass as the chunk of ice went sailing through it.

At last he fell into a troubled doze, with the bright light of the moon shining across the rug at the foot of the bed. But the doze did not last long, and soon some kind of a noise awoke him with a start.

He opened his eyes and his gaze wandered across the moon-lit room. Was he dreaming, or was that really a figure in white standing at the foot of his bed? With a shiver he ducked down and covered his head with the blankets.

For two or three minutes he lay quiet, expecting every instant to have something unusual happen. Then, with great caution, he pushed the blankets back and took another look.

There was nothing there!

"But I saw something," he told himself. "I am sure I saw something. What could it have been?"

Ah, that was the question. For over an hour he continued to lie awake, watching and listening. Nan was in the next little chamber and he was half of a mind to call her, but he was afraid she would call him a "'fraid-cat!" something he despised.

Bert had heard of ghosts and now he thought of all the ghost stories he could remember. Had the thing in white been a ghost? If so, where had it come from?

After a while he tried to dismiss the thing from his mind, but it was almost morning before he fell asleep again. This time he slept so soundly, however, that he did not rouse up until his mother came and shook him.

"Why, Bert, what makes you sleep so soundly this morning?" said Mrs. Bobbsey.

"I—I didn't get to sleep until late," he stammered. And then he added: "Mamma, do you believe in ghosts?"

"Why, of course not, Bert. What put that into your head?"

"I—I thought I saw a ghost last night."

"You must have been mistaken. There are no ghosts."

"But I saw *something*," insisted the boy.

"Where?"

"Right at the foot of the bed. It was all white."

"When was this?"

"Right in the middle of the night."

"Did you see it come in, or go out?"

"No, mamma. When I woke up it was standing there, and when I took a second look at it, it was gone."

"You must have been suffering from a nightmare, Bert," said Mrs. Bobbsey kindly. "You should not have eaten those nuts before going to bed."

"No, it wasn't a nightmare," said the boy.

He had but little to say while eating breakfast, but on the way to school he told Nan, while Freddie and Flossie listened also.

"Oh, Bert, supposing it was a real ghost?" cried Nan, taking a deep breath. "Why, I'd be scared out of my wits,—I know I'd be!"

"Mamma says there are no ghosts. But I saw something—I am sure of that."

"I don't want to see any ghostses," came from Flossie.

"Nor I," added Freddie. "Sam told about a ghost once that was as high as a tree an' had six heads, to eat bad boys and girls up. Did this have six heads, Bert?"

"No."

"How many heads did it have?"

"I don't know—one, I guess."

"And was it as high as a tree?" went on the inquisitive little fellow.

"Oh, it couldn't stand up in the room if it was as high as a tree," burst out Flossie.

"Could if it was a tiny *baby* tree," expostulated Freddie.

"It was about as high as that," said Bert, putting out his hand on a level with his shoulder. "I can't say how it looked, only it was white."

"Perhaps it was moonshine," suggested Nan, but at this Bert shook his head. He felt certain it had been more substantial than moonshine.

That day Danny Rugg came to school as usual. When questioned about his absence he said he had had a toothache. When Bert looked at him the big boy merely scowled, and no words passed between the pair.

Directly back of Lakeport was a long hill, used during the winter by all the boys and girls for coasting. After school Nan and Bert were allowed to go to this hill, in company with a number of their friends. They were admonished to come back before dark and promised faithfully to do so.

Among the boys there was a great rivalry as to who could go down the hill the fastest, and who could make his sled go the farthest after the bottom was reached.

"I'll try my sled against yours!" cried Charley Mason to Bert.

"Done!" returned Bert. "Are you going down alone, or are you going to carry somebody?"

"You must carry me down," insisted Nan.

"Then I'll take Nellie Parks," went on Charley.

Nellie was close at hand and soon the two sleds were side by side, with a girl on each. Bert and Charley stood behind.

"Are you ready?" asked Charley.

"Yes."

"Then go!"

Away went both lads, giving each sled a lively shove down the hill. Then each hopped aboard, and took hold of the rope with which to steer.

"A race! A race!" shouted those standing near.

"I think Charley will win!" said some.

"I think Bert will win!" said others.

"Oh, let us win if we can!" whispered Nan to her twin brother.

"I'll do my best, Nan," was the answer.

Down the long hill swept the two sleds, almost side by side. Each was rushing along at a lively rate of speed, and those aboard had to hold on tightly for fear of being jounced off.

"Whoop!" roared Charley. "Clear the track, for I am coming!"

"Make room for me!" sang out Bert. "We are bound to win!"

The bottom of the hill was almost reached when Charley's sled began to crawl a bit ahead.

"Oh, Bert, they are going to beat us after all," cried Nan disappointedly.

"I knew we'd beat you," cried Nellie Parks. "Charley's is the best sled on the hill."

"The race isn't over yet," said Bert.

His sled had been running in rather soft snow. Now he turned to where the coasting was better, and in a twinkling his sled shot forward until he was once more beside Charley and Nellie.

"Here we come!" shouted Bert. "Make room, I say! Make room."

On and on they went, and now the bottom of the hill was reached and they ran along a level stretch. Charley's sled began to slow up, but Bert's kept on and on until he had covered a hundred feet beyond where Charley had come to a stop.

"We've won!" cried Nan excitedly. "Oh, Bert, your sled is a wonder."

"So it is," he answered, with pride. "But it was a close race, wasn't it?"

When they came back to where Charley and Nellie stood they found Charley rather sulky.

"Nellie is heavier than Nan," said he. "It wasn't a fair race. Let us try it alone next time."

"I'm willing," answered Bert.

Coasting, and What Came of it

It was a long walk back to the top of the hill, but Nan and Bert did not mind it.

"So you won, did you?" said one of the boys to Bert. "Good enough."

"We are going to try it over again," put in Charley. "Come on."

In the crowd was Danny Rugg, who had a brand-new sled.

"I guess I can beat anybody!" cried Danny boastfully. "This new sled of mine is bang-up."

"What slang!" whispered Nan, to Bert. "If I were you I shouldn't race with him."

"I'm going to race with Charley," answered her twin brother, and took no notice of Danny's challenge.

Bert and Charley were soon ready for the test, and away they went amid a cheer from their friends.

"I think Charley will win this time," said Nellie.

"And I think that Bert will win," answered Nan.

"Oh, you think your brother is wonderful," sniffed Nellie, with a shrug of her shoulders.

"He is just as good as any boy," said Nan quickly.

Down the hill swept the two sleds, keeping side by side as before. They were but a foot apart, for each owner wished to keep on the hardest part of the slide.

"Keep on your side, Bert Bobbsey!" shouted Charley warningly.

"And you keep on yours, Charley Mason!" returned Bert.

All of the others on the hill had stopped coasting to witness the contest, but now with a whoop Danny Rugg swept forward with his new sled and came down the hill at top speed.

The bottom of the hill was barely reached when Charley's sled made an unexpected turn and crashed into Bert's, throwing Bert over on his side in the snow.

"What did you do that for?" demanded Bert angrily.

"I—I—didn't do it," stammered Charley. "I guess you turned into me."

"No, I didn't."

Bert arose and began to brush the snow from his clothes. As he did so he heard a rushing sound behind him and then came a crash as Danny Rugg ran into him. Down he went again and his sled had a runner completely broken off. Bert was hit in the ankle and badly bruised.

"Why didn't you get out of the way!" roared Danny Rugg roughly. "I yelled loud enough."

"Oh, my ankle!" groaned Bert. For the moment the wrecked sled was forgotten.

"I didn't touch your ankle," went on the big boy.

"You did so, Danny—at least, the point of your sled did," answered Bert.

"You ran into me in the first place," came from Charley.

"Oh, Charley, you know better than that." Bert tried to stand, but had to sit down. "Oh, my ankle!"

"It wasn't my fault," said Danny Rugg, and began to haul his sled away. Charley started to follow.

"Don't leave me, Charley," called out Bert. "I—I guess I can't walk."

Charley hesitated. Then, feeling in his heart that he was really responsible for running into Bert in the first place, he came back and helped Bert to his feet.

"The sled is broken," said Bert, surveying the wreck dismally.

"That was Danny's fault."

"Well, then, he ought to pay for having it fixed."

"He never pays for anything he breaks, Bert,—you know that."

Slowly and painfully Bert dragged himself and his broken sled to the top of the hill. Sharp, hot flashes of pain shooting through his bruised ankle. Nan ran to meet him.

"Oh, Bert, what is the matter? Are you hurt?" she asked.

"Yes,—Danny ran into me, and broke the sled."

"It wasn't my fault, I say!" blustered the big boy. "You had a right to get out of the way."

"It was your fault, Danny Rugg, and you will have to have my sled mended," cried Bert.

Throwing down the rope of his own sled, Danny advanced and doubled up his fists as if to fight.

"Don't you talk like that to me," he said surlily. "I don't like it."

Bert's ankle hurt too much for him to continue the quarrel. He felt himself growing dizzy and he fell back.

"Let us go home," whispered Nan.

"I'll ride you home if you can't walk," put in Charley, who was growing alarmed.

In the end Bert had to accept the offer, and home he went, with Charley and Nan pulling him and with the broken sled dragging on behind.

It was all he could do to get into the house, and as a consequence Mrs. Bobbsey was much alarmed. She took off his shoe and stocking and found the ankle scratched and swollen, and bathed it and bound it up.

"You must lie down on the sofa," she said. "Never mind the broken sled. Perhaps your papa can fix it when he comes home."

Bert detested playing the part of an invalid, but he soon discovered that keeping the ankle quiet felt much better than trying to walk around upon it. That night Mr. Bobbsey carried him up to bed, and he remained home for three days, when the ankle became as well as ever. The broken sled was sent to a nearby cabinet maker, and came back practically as good as new.

"You must not have anything to do with Danny Rugg," said Mrs. Bobbsey to her son. "He is very rough and ungentlemanly."

"I'll leave him alone, mamma, if he'll leave me alone," answered Bert.

During those days spent at home, Nan did her best to amuse her brother. As soon as she was out of school she came straight home, and read to him and played games. Nan was also learning to play on the piano and she played a number of tunes that he liked to hear. They were so much attached to each other that it did not seem natural for Nan to go out unless her twin brother could go out too.

The first snow storm had been followed by another, so that in the garden the snow lay deeper than ever. This was a great delight to Freddie and Flossie, who worked hard to build themselves a snow house. They enlisted the services of Sam, the stableman, who speedily piled up for them a heap of snow much higher than their heads.

"Now, chillun, dar am de house," said the colored man. "All yo' hab got to do is to clear out de insides." And then he went off to his work, after starting the hole for them.

Flossie wanted to divide the house into three rooms, "dining room, kitchen, and bedroom," as she said, but Freddie objected.

"'Taint big enough," said the little boy. "Make one big room and call it ev'rything."

"But we haven't got an *ev'rything*," said Flossie.

"Well, then, call it the parlor," said Freddie. "When it's done we can put in a carpet and two chairs for us to sit on."

It was hard work for such little hands to dig out the inside of the heap of snow, but they kept at it, and at last the hole was big enough for Freddie to crawl into.

"Oh, it's jess *beautiful*!" he cried, "Try it, Flossie!" And Flossie did try, and said the house was going to be perfect.

"Only we must have a bay window," she added. "And a curtain, just like mamma."

They continued to shovel away, and soon Freddie said he could almost stand up in the house. He was inside, shoveling out the snow, while his twin sister packed what he threw out on the outside, as Sam had told them to do.

"Where shall I put the bay window?" asked the little boy, presently.

"On this side," answered Flossie, pointing with the shovel she held.

At once Freddie began to dig a hole through the side of the pile of snow.

"Be careful, or the house will come down!" cried Flossie, all at once, and hardly had she spoken when down came the whole top of the snow pile and poor Freddie was buried completely out of sight!

Freddie and Flossie's Snow House

"Freddie! Freddie!" shrieked Flossie, when she saw her twin brother disappear. "Do come out!"

But Freddie could not come out, and when, after a few seconds he did not show himself, she ran toward the kitchen door, screaming at the top of her breath.

"Oh, Dinah! Dinah! Freddie is buried! Freddie is buried!"

"Wot's dat yo' say, Flossie?" demanded the cook, coming to the door.

"Freddie is buried. The ceiling of the snow house came down on him!"

"Gracious sakes alive, chile!" burst out Dinah, and without waiting to put anything on her head she rushed forth into the garden. "Gib me dat shovel quick! He'll be stuffocated fo' yo' know it."

She began to dig away at the pile of snow, and presently uncovered one of Freddie's lower limbs. Then she dropped the shovel and tugged away at the limb and presently brought Freddie to view, just as Mrs. Bobbsey and Nan appeared on the scene.

"What in the world is the matter?" questioned Mrs. Bobbsey, in alarm.

"Dat chile dun gwine an' buried himself alive," responded the colored cook. "De roof of de snow house cabed in on him, pooh dear! He's 'most stuffocated!"

In the meantime Freddie was gasping for breath. Then he looked at the wreck of the snow house and set up a tremendous roar of dismay.

"Oh, Flossie, it's all spoilt! The bay window an' all!"

"Never mind, Freddie dear," said his mother, taking him. "Be thankful that you were not suffocated, as Dinah says."

"Yes, but Flossie and me were makin' an *ev'rything* house, with a parlor, an' a bay window, an' *ev'rything*. I didn't want it to fall down." Freddie was still gasping, but now he struggled to the ground. "Want to build it up again," he added.

"I am afraid you'll get into trouble again, Freddie."

"No, I won't, mamma. Do let us build it up again," pleaded the little fellow.

"I kin watch dem from de doah," suggested Dinah.

"Let me help them, mamma," put in Nan. "Bert is reading a book, so he won't want me for a while."

"Very well, Nan, you may stay with them. But all of you be careful," said Mrs. Bobbsey.

After that the building of the snow house was started all over again. The pile of snow was packed down as hard as possible, and Nan made Flossie and Freddie do the outside work while she crept inside, and cut around the ceiling and the bay window just as the others wanted. It was great sport, and when the snow house was finished it was large enough and strong enough for all of them to enter with safety.

"To-night I'll poah some water ober dat house," said Sam. "Dat will make de snow as hard as ice." This was done, and the house remained in the garden until spring came. Later on Bert built an addition to it, which he called the library, and in this he put a bench and a shelf on which he placed some old magazines and story papers. In the main part of the snow house Freddie and Flossie at first placed an old rug and two blocks of wood for chairs, and a small bench for a table. Then, when Flossie grew tired of the house, Freddie turned it into a stable, in which he placed his rocking-horse. Then he brought out his iron fire engine, and used the place for a fire-house, tying an old dinner bell on a stick, stuck over the doorway. *Dong! dong!* would go the bell, and out he would rush with his little engine and up the garden path, looking for a fire.

"Let us play you are a reg'lar fireman," said Flossie, on seeing this. "You must live in the fire-house, and I must be your wife and come to see you with the baby." And she dressed up in a long skirt and paid him a visit, with her best doll on her arm. Freddie pretended to be very glad to see her, and embraced the baby. But a moment later he made the bell ring, and throwing the baby to her rushed off again with his engine.

"That wasn't very nice," pouted Flossie. "Dorothy might have fallen in the snow."

"Can't help it," answered Freddie. "A fireman can't stop for anything."

"But—but—he doesn't have to throw his baby away, does he?" questioned Flossie, with wide open eyes.

"Yes, he does,—*ev'rything.*"

"But—but supposing he is—is eating his dinner?"

"He has to throw it away, Flossie. Oh, it's awful hard to be a real fireman."

"Would he have to throw his jam away, and his pie?"

"Yes."

"Then I wouldn't be a fireman, not for a—a house full of gold!" said Flossie, and marched back into the house with her doll.

Flossie's dolls were five in number. Dorothy was her pride, and had light hair and blue eyes, and three dresses, one of real lace. The next was Gertrude, a short doll with black eyes and hair and a traveling dress that was very cute. Then came Lucy, who had lost one arm, and Polly, who had lost both an arm and a leg. The fifth doll was Jujube, a colored boy, dressed in a fiery suit of red, with a blue cap and real rubber boots. This doll had come from Sam and Dinah and had been much admired at first, but was now taken out only when all the others went too.

"He doesn't really belong to the family, you know," Flossie would explain to her friends. "But I have to keep him, for mamma says there is no colored orphan asylum for dolls. Besides, I don't think Sam and Dinah would like to see their doll child in an asylum." The dolls were all kept in a row in a big bureau drawer at the top of the house, but Flossie always took pains to separate Jujube from the rest by placing the cover of a pasteboard box between them.

With so much snow on the ground it was decided by the boys of that neighborhood to build a snow fort, and this work was undertaken early on the following Saturday morning. Luckily, Bert was by that time well enough to go out and he did his fair share of the labor, although being careful not to injure the sore ankle.

The fort was built at the top of a small hill in a large open lot. It was made about twenty feet square and the wall was as high as the boys' heads and over a foot thick. In the middle was gathered a big pile of snow, and into this was stuck a flag-pole from which floated a nice flag loaned by a boy named Ralph Blake.

"Let us divide into two parties of soldiers," said Ralph. "One can defend the fort and the others can attack it."

"Hurrah! just the thing!" cried Bert. "When shall the battle begin?"

The boys talked it over, and it was decided to have the battle come off after lunch.

The boys went home full of enthusiasm, and soon the news spread that a real soldiers' battle was to take place at the lot.

"Oh, Bert, can't I go and look on?" asked Nan.

"I want to go, too," put in Flossie.

"Can't I be a soldier?" asked Freddie. "I can make snowballs, and throw 'em, too."

"No, Freddie, you are too little to be a soldier," answered Bert. "But you can all come and look on, if you wish."

After lunch the boys began to gather quickly, until over twenty were present. Many girls and a few grown folks were also there, who took places out of harm's way.

"Now, remember," said a gentleman who was placed in charge. "No icy snowballs and no stones."

"We'll remember, Mr. Potter," cried the young soldiers.

The boys were speedily divided into two parties, one to attack and one to defend the fort. It fell to Bert's lot to be one of the attacking party. Without loss of time each party began to make all the snowballs it could. The boys who remained in the fort kept out of sight behind the walls, while the attacking party moved to the back of the barn at the corner of the big lot.

"Are you all ready?" shouted Mr. Potter presently.

A yell of assent came from nearly all of the young soldiers.

"Very well, then; the battle may begin."

Some of the boys had brought horns along, and now a rousing blast came from behind the barn and then from the snow fort.

"Come on and capture the fort!" cried Bert, and led the way, with his arms full of snowballs.

There was a grand cheer and up the hill rushed the young soldiers, ready to capture the snow fort no matter what the cost.

Fun on the Ice

"Oh, the fight is going to start!" cried Nan, in high excitement. "See them coming up the hill!"

"Will they shoot?" asked Flossie, just a bit nervously.

"Course they won't shoot," answered Freddie. "Can't shoot snowballs. Ain't got no powder in."

The attacking party was still a good distance from the fort when those inside let fly a volley of snowballs. But the snowballs did not reach their mark, and still the others came up the hill.

"Now then, give it to them!" cried Bert, and let fly his first snowball, which landed on the top of the fort's wall. Soon the air was full of snowballs, flying one way and another. Many failed to do any damage, but some went true, and soon Bert received a snowball full in the breast and another in the shoulder. Then he slipped and fell and his own snowballs were lost.

The attacking party got to within fifty feet of the fort, but then the ammunition gave out and they were forced to retreat, which they did in quick order.

"Hurrah! they can't take the fort!" cried those inside of the stronghold, and blew their horns more wildly than ever. But their own ammunition was low and they made other snowballs as quickly as they could, using the pile of snow in the middle of the fort for that purpose.

Back of the barn the attacking party held a consultation.

"I've got a plan," said a boy named Ned Brown. "Let us divide into two parties and one move on the fort from the front and the other from the back. Then, if they attack one party, the other party can sneak in and climb over the fort wall and capture the flag."

"All right, let us do that," said Bert.

Waiting until each boy had a dozen or more snowballs, half of the attacking force moved away along a fence until the rear of the fort was gained. Then, with another cheer, all set out for the fort.

It was a grand rush and soon the air was once more filled with snowballs, much to the delight of the spectators, who began to cheer both sides.

"Oh, I hope they get into the fort this time," said Nan.

"I hope they don't," answered another girl, who had a brother in the fort.

Inside the fort the boys were having rather a hard time of it. They were close together, and a snowball coming over the walls was almost certain to hit one or another. More than this, the pile of snow around the flag was growing small, so that the flag was in great danger of toppling over.

Up the two sides of the hill came the invaders, Bert leading the detachment that was to attack the rear. He was hit again, but did not falter, and a moment later found himself at the very wall.

"Get back there!" roared a boy from the fort and threw a large lump of soft snow directly into his face. But Bert threw the lump back and the boy slipped and fell flat. Then, amid a perfect shower of snowballs, Bert and two other boys fairly tumbled into the fort.

"Defend the flag! Defend the flag!" was the rallying cry of the fort defenders, and they gathered around the flag. The struggle was now a hand-to-hand one, in which nothing but soft snow was used, and nearly every boy had his face washed.

"Get back there!" roared Danny Rugg, who was close to the flag, but as he spoke two boys shoved him down on his face in the snow, and the next moment Bert and another boy of the invading party had the flag and was carrying it away in triumph.

"The fort has fallen!" screamed Nan, and clapped her hands.

"Hurrah!" shouted Freddie. "The—the forters are beaten, aren't they?"

"Yes, Freddie."

A cheer was given for those who had captured the fort. Then some of the boys began to dance on the top of the walls, and down they came, one after another, until the fort was in ruins, and the great contest came to an end.

"It was just splendid!" said Nan to Bert, on the way home. "Just like a real battle."

"Only the band didn't play," put in Freddie disappointedly. "Real soldiers have a band. They don't play fish-horns."

"Oh, Freddie!" cried Flossie. "They weren't fish-horns. They were Christmas horns."

"It's all the same. I like a band, with a big, fat bass-drum."

"We'll have the band next time—just for your benefit, Freddie," said Bert.

He was tired out and glad to rest when they got home. More than this, some of the snow had gotten down his back, so he had to dry himself by sitting with his back to the sitting-room heater.

"Danny Rugg was terribly angry that we captured the fort," said he. "He is looking for the boys who threw him on his face."

"It served him right," answered Nan, remembering the trouble over the broken show window.

The second fall of snow was followed by steady cold weather and it was not long before the greater part of Lake Metoka was frozen over. As soon as this happened nearly all of the boys and girls took to skating, so that sledding and snowballing were, for the time being, forgotten.

Both Nan and Bert had new skates, given to them the Christmas before, and each was impatient to go on the ice, but Mrs. Bobbsey held them back until she thought it would be safe.

"You must not go too far from shore," said she. "I understand the ice in the middle of the lake, and at the lower end, is not as firm as it might be."

Freddie and Flossie wanted to watch the skating, and Nan took them to their father's lumber yard. Here was a small office directly on the lake front, where they could see much that was going on and still be under the care of an old workman around the yards.

Nan could not skate very well, but Bert could get along nicely, and he took hold of his twin sister's hand, and away they went gliding over the smooth ice much to their combined delight.

"Some day I am going to learn how to do fancy skating," said Bert. "The Dutch roll, and spread the eagle, and all that."

"There is Mr. Gifford," said Nan. "Let us watch him."

The gentleman mentioned was a fine skater and had once won a medal for making fancy figures on the ice. They watched him for a long while and so did many of the others present.

"It's beautiful to skate like that," cried Nan, when they skated away. "It's just like knowing how to dance everything."

"Only better," said Bert, who did not care for dancing at all.

Presently Nan found some girls to skate with and then Bert went off among the boys. The girls played tag and had great fun, shrieking at the top of their lungs as first one was "it" and then another. It was hard work for Nan to catch the older girls, who could skate better, but easy enough to catch those of her own age and experience on the ice.

The boys played tag, too, and "snapped the whip," as it is termed. All of the boys would join hands in a long line and then skate off as fast as they could. Then the boy on one end, called the snapper, would stop and pull the others around in a big curve. This would make the boys on the end of the line skate very fast, and sometimes they would go down, to roll over and over on the ice. Once Bert was at the end and down he went, to slide a long distance, when he bumped into a gentleman who was skating backwards and over went the man with a crash that could be heard a long distance off.

"Hi! you young rascal!" roared the man, trying to scramble up. "What do you mean by bowling me over like that?"

"Excuse me, but I didn't mean to do it," answered Bert, and lost no time in getting out of the gentleman's way. The gentleman was very angry and left the ice, grumbling loudly to himself.

Down near the lower end of Mr. Bobbsey's lumber yard some young men were building an ice-boat. Bert and Charley Mason watched this work with interest. "Let us make an ice-boat," said Charley. "I can get an old bed-sheet for a sail, if you will get your father to give you the lumber."

"I'll try," answered Bert, and it was agreed that the ice-boat should be built during the following week, after school.

Freddie Loses Himself

Christmas was now but four weeks away, and the stores of Lakeport had their windows filled with all sort of nice things for presents. Nan and Bert had gazed into the windows a number of times, and even walked through the one big department store of which the town boasted, and they had told Freddie and Flossie of many of the things to be seen.

"Oh, I want to see them, too!" cried Flossie, and begged her mother to take her along the next time she went out.

"I want to go, too," put in Freddie. "Bert says there are *sixteen* rocking horses all in a row, with white and black tails. I want to see them."

"I am going to the stores to-morrow," answered Mrs. Bobbsey. "You can go with me, after school. It will be better to go now than later on, when the places are filled with Christmas shoppers."

The twins were in high glee, and Freddie said he was going to spend the twenty-five cents he had been saving up for several months.

"Let us buy mamma something for Christmas," said Flossie, who had the same amount of money.

"What shall we buy?"

That question was a puzzling one. Flossie thought a nice doll would be the right thing, while Freddie thought an automobile that could be wound up and made to run around the floor would be better. At last both consulted Nan.

"Oh, mamma doesn't want a doll," said Nan. "And she ought to have a real automobile, not a tin one."

"Can't buy a real auto'bile," said Freddie. "Real auto'biles cost ten dollars, or more."

"I'll tell you what to do," went on Nan. "You buy her a little bottle of cologne, Freddie, and you, Flossie, can buy her a nice handkerchief."

"I'll buy her a big bottle of cologne," said Freddie. "That big!" and he placed his hands about a foot apart.

"And I'll get a real lace handkerchief," added Flossie.

"You'll have to do the best you can," said practical Nan, and so it was agreed.

When they left home each child had the money tucked away in a pocket. They went in the family sleigh, with Sam as a driver. The first stop was at Mr. Ringley's shoe store, where Mrs. Bobbsey purchased each of the twins a pair of shoes. It may be added here, that the broken window glass had long since been replaced by the shoe dealer, and his show window looked as attractive as ever.

"I heard you had a window broken not long ago," said Mrs. Bobbsey, when paying for her purchases.

"Yes, two bad boys broke the window," answered the shoe dealer.

"Who were they?"

"I couldn't find out. But perhaps I'll learn some day, and then I mean to have them arrested," said Mr. Ringley. "The broken glass ruined several pairs of shoes that were in the window." And then he turned away to wait on another customer.

Soon the large department store was reached and Mrs. Bobbsey let Freddie and Flossie take their time in looking into the several windows. One was full of dolls, which made the little girl gape in wonder and delight.

"Oh, mamma, what a flock of dolls!" she cried. "Must be 'bout ten millions of them, don't you think so?"

"Hardly that many, Flossie; but there are a good many."

"And, oh, mamma, what pretty dresses! I wish I had that doll with the pink silk and the big lace hat," added the little girl.

"Do you think that is the nicest, Flossie?"

"Indeed, indeed I do," answered the little miss. "It's too lovely for anything. Can't we get it and take it home?"

"No, dear; but you had better ask Santa Claus to send it to you," continued her mother with a smile.

Some wooden soldiers and building blocks caught Freddie's eye, and for the time being his favorite fire engines were forgotten.

"I want wooden soldiers," he said. "Can set 'em up in a row, with the sword-man in front, an' the man with the drum."

"Perhaps Santa Claus will bring you some soldiers in your stocking, Freddie."

"Stocking ain't big enough—want big ones, like that," and he pointed with his chubby hand.

"Well, let us wait and see what Santa Claus can do," said Mrs. Bobbsey.

Inside of the store was a candy counter near the doorway, and there was no peace for Mrs. Bobbsey until she had purchased some chocolate drops for Flossie, and a long peppermint cane for Freddie. Then they walked around, down one aisle and up another, admiring the many things which were displayed.

"Bert said they had a lavater," said Freddie presently. "Mamma, I want to go in the lavater."

"Lavater?" repeated Mrs. Bobbsey, with a puzzled look. "Why, Freddie, what do you mean?"

"He means the stairs that runs up and down on a big rope," put in Flossie.

"Oh, the elevator," said the mother. "Very well, you shall both ride in the elevator."

It was great sport to ride to the third story of the store, although the swift way in which the elevator moved made the twins gasp a little.

"Let us go down again," said Freddie. "It's ever so much nicer than climbing the stairs."

"I wish to make a few purchases first," answered the mother.

She had come to buy a rug for the front hallway, and while she was busy in the rug and carpet department she allowed the twins to look at a number of toys which were located at the other end of the floor.

For a while Freddie and Flossie kept close together, for there was quite a crowd present and they felt a little afraid. But then Flossie discovered a counter where all sorts of things for dolls were on sale and she lingered there, to look at the dresses, and hats, and underwear, and shoes and stockings, and chairs, trunks, combs and brushes, and other goods.

"Oh, my, I must have some of those things for my dolls," she said, half aloud. There was a trunk she thought perfectly lovely and it was marked 39 cents. "Not so very much," she thought.

When Freddie got around to where the elevator was, it was just coming up again with another load of people. As he had not seen it go down he concluded that he must go down by way of the stairs if he wanted another ride.

"I'll get a ride all by myself," he thought, and as quickly as he could, he slipped down first one pair of stairs and then another, to the ground floor of the store. Then he saw another stairs, and soon was in the basement of the department store.

Here was a hardware department with a great number of heavy toys, and soon he was looking at a circular railroad track upon which ran a real locomotive and three cars. This was certainly a wonderful toy, and Freddie could not get his eyes off of it.

In moving around the basement of the store, Freddie grew hopelessly mixed up, and when he started to look for the elevator or the stairs, he walked to the storage room. He was too timid to ask his way out and soon found himself among great rows of boxes and barrels. Then he made a turn or two and found himself in another room, filled with empty boxes and casks, some partly filled with straw and excelsior. There was a big wooden door to this room, and while he was inside the door shut with a bang and the catch fell into place.

"Oh, dear, I wish I was back with mamma," he thought, and drew a long and exceedingly sober breath. "I don't like it here at all."

Just then a little black kitten came toward him and brushed up affectionately. Freddie caught the kitten and sat down for a moment to pet it. He now felt sleepy and in a few minutes his eyes closed and his head began to nod. Then in a minute more he went sound asleep.

Long before this happened Mrs. Bobbsey found Flossie and asked her where Freddie was. The little girl could not tell, and the mother began a diligent search. The floor-walkers in the big store aided her, but it was of no avail. Freddie could not be found, and soon it was time to close up the establishment for the day. Almost frantic with fear, Mrs. Bobbsey telephoned to her husband, telling him of what had occurred and asked him what had best be done.

Lost and Found

When Freddie woke up all was very, very dark around him. At first he thought he was at home, and he called out for somebody to pull up the curtain that he might see.

But nobody answered him, and all he heard was a strange purring, close to his ear. He put up his hand and touched the little black kitten, which was lying close to his face. He had tumbled back in the straw and this had proved a comfortable couch upon which to take a nap.

"Oh, dear me, I'll have to get back to mamma!" he murmured, as he struggled up and rubbed his eyes. "What can make it so awful dark? They ought to light the gas. Nobody can buy things when it's so dark as this."

The darkness did not please him, and he was glad to have the black kitten for a companion. With the kitten in his arms he arose to his feet and walked a few steps. Bump! he went into a big box. Then he went in another direction and stumbled over a barrel.

"Mamma! Mamma!" he cried out. "Mamma, where are you?"

No answer came back to this call, and his own voice sounded so queer to him that he soon stopped. He hugged the kitten tighter than ever.

He was now greatly frightened and it was all he could do to keep back the tears. He knew it must be night and that the great store must be closed up.

"They have all gone home and left me here alone," he thought. "Oh, what shall I do?"

He knew the night was generally very long and he did not wish to remain in the big, lonely building until morning.

Still hugging the kitten, he felt his way around until he reached the big wooden door. The catch came open with ease, and once more he found himself in that part of the basement used for hardware and large mechanical toys. But the toy locomotive had ceased to run and all was very silent. Only a single gas jet flickered overhead, and this cast fantastic shadows which made the little boy think of ghosts and hobgoblins. One mechanical toy had a very large head on it, and this seemed to grin and laugh at him as he looked at it.

"Mamma!" he screamed again. "Oh, mamma, why don't you come?"

He listened and presently he heard footsteps overhead.

"Who's there?" came in the heavy voice of a man.

The voice sounded so unnatural that Freddie was afraid to answer. Perhaps the man might be a burglar come to rob the store.

"I say, who's there?" repeated the voice. "Answer me."

There was a minute of silence, and then Freddie heard the footsteps coming slowly down the stairs. The man had a lantern in one hand and a club in the other.

Not knowing what else to do, Freddie crouched behind a counter. His heart beat loudly, and he had dim visions of burglars who might have entered the big store to rob it. If he was discovered, there was no telling what such burglars might do with him.

"Must have been the cat," murmured the man on the stairs. He reached the basement floor and swung his lantern over his head. "Here, kittie, kittie, kittie!" he called.

"Meow!" came from the black kitten, which was still in Freddie's arms. Then the man looked in that direction.

"Hullo!" he exclaimed, starting in amazement. "What are you doing here? Are you alone?"

"Oh, please, I want my mamma!" cried Freddie.

"You want your mamma?" repeated the man. "Say!" he went on suddenly. "Are you the kid that got lost this afternoon, youngster?"

"I guess I did get lost," answered Freddie. He saw that the man had a kindly face and this made him a bit braver. "I walked around and sat down over there—in the straw—and went to sleep."

"Well, I never!" cried the man. "And have you been down here ever since?"

"Yes, sir. But I don't want to stay—I want to go home."

"All right, you shall go. But this beats me!"

"Are you the man who owns the store?" questioned Freddie curiously.

At this the man laughed. "No; wish I did. I'm the night watchman. Let me see, what is your name?"

"Freddie Bobbsey. My papa owns the lumber yard."

"Oh, yes, I remember now. Well, Freddie, I reckon your papa will soon come after you. All of 'em are about half crazy, wondering what has become of you."

The night watchman led the way to the first floor of the department store and Freddie followed, still clutching the black kitten, which seemed well content to remain with him.

"I'll telephone to your papa," said the watchman, and going into one of the offices he rang the bell and called up the number of the Bobbsey residence.

In the meantime Mrs. Bobbsey and the others of the family were almost frantic with grief and alarm. Mr. Bobbsey had notified the police and the town had been searched thoroughly for some trace of the missing boy.

"Perhaps they have stolen Freddie away!" said Nan, with the tears starting to her eyes. "Some gypsies were in town, telling fortunes. I heard one of the girls at school tell about it."

"Oh, the bad gypsies!" cried Flossie, and gave a shudder. The idea that Freddie might have been carried off by the gypsies was truly terrifying.

Mr. Bobbsey had been out a dozen times to the police headquarters and to the lake front. A report had come in that a boy looking like Freddie had been seen on the ice early in the evening, and he did not know but what the little fellow might have wandered in that direction.

When the telephone bell rang Mr. Bobbsey had just come in from another fruitless search. Both he and his wife ran to the telephone.

"Hullo!" came over the wire. "Is this Mr. Bobbsey's house?"

"It is," answered the gentleman quickly. "What do you want? Have you any news?"

"I've found your little boy, sir," came back the reply. "He is safe and sound with me."

"And who are you?"

"The night watchman at the department store. He went to sleep here, that's all."

At this news all were overjoyed.

"Let me speak to him," said Mrs. Bobbsey eagerly. "Freddie dear, are you there?" she asked.

"Yes, mamma," answered Freddie, into the telephone. "And I want to come home."

"You shall, dear. Papa shall come for you at once."

"Oh, he's found! He's found!" shrieked Nan. "Aren't you glad, Bert?"

"Of course I am," answered Bert. "But I can't understand how he happened to go to sleep in such a lively store as that."

"He must have walked around until he got tired," replied Nan. "You know Freddie can drop off to sleep very quickly when he gets tired."

As soon as possible Mr. Bobbsey drove around to the department store in his sleigh. The watchman and Freddie were on the look-out for him, the little boy with the kitten still in his arms.

"Oh, papa!" cried Freddie. "I am so glad you have come! I—I don't want to go to sleep here again!"

The watchman's story was soon told, and Mr. Bobbsey made him happy by presenting him with a two-dollar bill.

"The little chap would have been even more lonely if it hadn't been for the kitten," said the man. "He wanted to keep the thing, so I told him to do it."

"And I'm going to," said Freddie proudly. "It's just the dearest kitten in the world." And keep the kitten he did. It soon grew to be a big, fat cat and was called Snoop.

By the time home was reached, Freddie was sleepy again. But he speedily woke up when his mamma and the others embraced him, and then he had to tell the story of his adventure from end to end.

"I do not know as I shall take you with me again," said Mrs. Bobbsey. "You have given us all a great scare."

"Oh, mamma, I won't leave you like that again," cried Freddie quickly. "Don't like to be in the dark 'tall," he added.

"Oh, it must have been awful," said Flossie. "Didn't you see any—any ghosts?"

"Barrels of them," said Freddie, nodding his head sleepily. "But they didn't touch me. Guess they was sleepy, just like me." And then he dropped off and had to be put to bed; and that was the end of this strange happening.

The Cruise of the "Ice Bird"

The building of the ice boat by Bert and Charley Mason interested Nan almost as much as it did the boys, and nearly every afternoon she went down to the lumber yard to see how the work was getting along.

Mr. Bobbsey had given Bert just the right kind of lumber, and had a man at the saw-mill saw the sticks and boards to a proper size. He also gave his son some ropes and a pair of old iron runners from a discarded sleigh, so that all Charley had to provide was the bed-sheet already mentioned, for a sail.

The two boys worked with a will, and by Thursday evening had the ice boat completed. They christened the craft the *Ice Bird*, and Bert insisted upon it that his father come and see her.

"You have certainly done very well," said Mr. Bobbsey. "This looks as if you were cut out for a builder, Bert."

"Well, I'd like to build big houses and ships first-rate," answered Bert.

The sail was rigged with the help of an old sailor who lived down by the lake shore, and on Friday afternoon Bert and Charley took a short trip. The *Ice Bird* behaved handsomely, much to the boys' satisfaction.

"She's a dandy!" cried Bert. "How she can whiz before the wind."

"You must take me out soon," said Nan.

"I will," answered Bert.

The chance to go out with Bert came sooner than expected. On Monday morning Mrs. Mason made up her mind to pay a distant relative a visit and asked Charley if he wished to go along. The boy wanted to see his cousins very much and said yes; and thus the ice boat was left in Bert's sole charge.

"I'll take you out Monday afternoon, after school," said Bert to his twin sister.

"Good!" cried Nan. "Let us go directly school is out, so as to have some good, long rides."

Four o'clock in the afternoon found them at the lake shore. It was a cloudy day with a fair breeze blowing across the lake.

"Now you sit right there," said Bert, as he pointed to a seat in the back of the boat. "And hold on tight or you'll be thrown overboard."

Nan took the seat mentioned, and her twin brother began to hoist the mainsail of the *Ice Bird*. It ran up easily, and caught by the wind the craft began to skim over the surface of the lake like a thing of life.

"Oh, but this is lovely!" cried Nan gleefully. "How fast the boat spins along!"

"I wish there were more ice boats around," answered Bert. "We might then have a race."

"Oh, it is pleasure enough just to sail around," said Nan.

Many other boys and girls wished a ride on the ice boat, and in the end Bert carried a dozen or more across the lake and back. It was rather hard work tacking against the wind, but the old sailor had taught him how it might be done, and he got along fairly well. When the ice boat got stuck all the boys and girls got off and helped push the craft along.

"It is 'most supper time," said Nan, as the whistle at the saw-mill blew for six o'clock. "We'll have to go home soon, Bert."

"Oh, let us take one more trip," pleaded her twin brother.

The other boys and girls had gone and they were left alone. To please Bert, Nan consented, and their course was changed so that the *Ice Bird* might move down the lake instead of across.

It had grown dark and the stars which might have shone in the sky were hidden by heavy clouds.

"Not too far now, remember," said Nan.

The wind had veered around and was blowing directly down the lake, so, almost before they knew it, the *Ice Bird* was flying along at a tremendous rate of speed. Nan had to hold on tight for fear of falling off, and had to hold her hat, too, for fear that would be blown away.

"Oh, Bert, this is too fast!" she gasped, catching her breath.

"It's just glorious, Nan!" he cried. "Just hold on, it won't hurt you."

"But—but how are we to get back?"

Bert had not thought of that, and at the question his face fell a little.

"Oh, we'll get back somehow," he said evasively.

"You had better turn around now."

"Let us go just a little bit further, Nan," he pleaded.

When at last he started to turn back he found himself unable to do so. The wind was blowing fiercely and the *Ice Bird* swept on before it in spite of all he could do.

"Bert! Bert! Oh, why don't you turn around?" screamed Nan. She had to scream in order to make herself heard.

"I—I can't," he faltered. "She won't come around."

Nan was very much frightened, and it must be confessed that Bert was frightened too. He hauled on the sail and on the steering gear, and at last the *Ice Bird* swung partly around. But instead of returning up the lake the craft headed for the western shore, and in a few minutes they struck some lumpy ice and some snow and dirt, and both were thrown out at full length, while the *Ice Bird* was tipped up on one side.

Bert picked himself up without difficulty and then went to Nan's aid. She lay deep in the snow, but fortunately was not hurt. Both gazed at the tipped-up ice boat in very great dismay.

"Bert, whatever shall we do now?" asked Nan, after a spell of silence. "We'll never get home at all!"

"Oh, yes, we shall," he said, bravely enough, but with a sinking heart. "We've got to get home, you know."

"But the ice boat is upset, and it's so dark I can't see a thing."

"I think I can right the ice boat. Anyway, I can try."

Doing his best to appear brave, Bert tried to shove the *Ice Bird* over to her original position. But the craft was too heavy for him, and twice she fell back, the second time coming close to smashing his toes.

"Look out, or you'll hurt your foot," cried Nan. "Let me help you."

Between them they presently got the craft right side up. But now the wind was blowing directly from the lake, so to get the *Ice Bird* out on the ice again was beyond them. Every time they shoved the craft out the wind drove her back.

"Oh, dear, I guess we have got to stay here after all!" sighed Bert, at last.

"Not stay here all night, I hope!" gasped Nan. "That would be worse than to stay in the store, as Freddie did."

It began to snow. At first the flakes were but few, but soon they came down thicker and thicker, blotting out the already darkened landscape.

"Let us walk home," suggested Nan. "That will be better than staying out here in the snow storm."

"It's a long walk. If only we had brought our skates." But alas! neither had thought to bring skates, and both pairs were in the office at the lumber yard.

"I don't think we had better walk home over the ice," said Bert, after another pause. "We may get all turned around and lost. Let us walk over to the Hopedale road."

"I wish we had some crullers, or something," said Nan, who was growing hungry. They had each had a cruller on leaving home, but had eaten them up before embarking on the ice-boat voyage.

"Please don't speak of them, Nan. You make me feel awfully hollow," came from her twin brother. And the way he said this was so comical it made her laugh in spite of her trouble.

The laugh put them both in better spirits, and leaving the *Ice Bird* where she lay, they set off through the snow in the direction of the road which ran from Lakeport to the village of Hopedale, six miles away.

"It will take us over an hour to get home," said Nan.

"Yes, and I suppose we'll catch it for being late," grumbled Bert. "Perhaps we won't get any supper."

"Oh, I know mamma won't scold us after she finds out why we were late, Bert."

They had to cross a pasture and climb a fence before the road was reached. Here was an old cow-shed and they stood in the shelter of this for a moment, out of the way of the wind and driving snow.

"Hark!" cried Bert as they were on the point of continuing their journey.

"It's a dog!" answered Nan. "Oh, Bert, he is coming this way. Perhaps he is savage!"

They listened and could hear the dog plainly. He was barking furiously and coming toward them as fast as he could travel. Soon they made out his black form looming into view through the falling snow.

Tige—playing Theater

Nan dearly loved the dogs with which she was well acquainted, but she was in great terror of strange animals, especially if they barked loudly and showed a disposition to bite.

"Bert! Bert! what shall we do?" she gasped as she clung to her twin brother's arm.

Bert hardly knew what to say, for he himself did not like a biting dog. He looked around for a stick or a stone, and espied the doorway to the cow-shed. It was open.

"Let us get into the shed," he said quickly. "Perhaps we can close the door and keep the dog out."

Into the shed sprang Nan and her twin brother after her. The dog was almost upon them when Bert banged the door in his face. At once the animal stopped short and began to bark more furiously than ever.

"Do you—you think he can get in at the window?" faltered Nan. She was so scared she could scarcely speak.

"I don't know, I'm sure. If you'll stand by the door, Nan, I'll try to guard the window."

Nan threw her form against the door and held it as hard as if a giant were outside trying to force it in. Bert felt around the empty shed and picked up the handle of a broken spade. With this in hand he stalked over to the one little window which was opposite the door.

"Are there any cows here?" asked Nan. It was so dark she could see next to nothing.

"No cows here, I guess," answered Bert. "This building is 'most ready to tumble down."

The dog outside was barking still. Once in a while he would stop to catch his breath and then he would continue as loudly as ever. He scratched at the door with his paw, which made Nan shiver from head to feet.

"He is trying to work his way in," she cried.

"If he does that, I'll hit him with this," answered her twin brother, and brandished the spade handle over his head. He watched the window closely and wondered what they had best do if the dog leaped straight through and attacked them in the dark.

The barking continued for over quarter of an hour. To Nan and Bert it seemed hours and hours. Then came a call from a distance.

"Hi, Tige, what's the matter? Have you spotted a tramp in the shed?"

"Help! help!" called out Bert. "Call off your dog!"

"A tramp, sure enough," said the man who was coming toward the cow-shed.

"I am not a tramp," answered Bert. "And my sister isn't a tramp, either."

"What's that? You've got your sister with you? Open the door."

"Please, we are afraid of the dog," came from Nan. "He came after us and we ran into the shed for shelter."

"Oh, that's it?" The farmer gave a short laugh. "Well, you needn't be skeert! Tige won't hurt ye none."

"Are you sure of that?" put in Bert. "He seems to be very savage."

"I won't let him touch ye."

Thus assured Nan opened the door and followed Bert outside. At a word from the farmer Tige stopped barking and began to wag his tail.

"That dog wouldn't hurt nobody, 'ceptin' he was attacked, or if a person tried to git in my house," said Farmer Sandborn. "He's a very nice fellow, he is, and likes boys and gals fust-rate; don't ye, Tige?" And the dog wagged his tail harder than ever, as if he understood every word.

"I—I was so scared," said Nan.

"May I ask what you be a-doin' on the road all alone and in this snowstorm?"

"We are going home," answered Bert, and then explained how they had been ice-boating and what had happened on the lake.

"I do declare!" cried Farmer Sandborn. "So the boat up an' run away with ye, did she? Contrary critter, eh!" And he began to laugh. "Who be you?"

"I am Bert Bobbsey and this is my twin sister Nan."

"Oh, yes, I know now. You're one pair o' the Bobbsey twins, as they call 'em over to Lakeport. I've heard Sary speak o' ye. Sary's my wife."

The farmer ran his hand through his thick beard. "You can't tramp home in this storm."

"Oh, we must get home," said Nan. "What will mamma say? She will think we are killed, or drowned, or something,—and she isn't over the scare she got when Freddie was lost."

"I'll take you back to town in my sleigh," said Farmer Sandborn. "I was going to town for some groceries to-morrow morning, but I might just as well go now, while the roads are open. They'll be all closed up ag'in by daylight, if this storm keeps up."

He led the way down the road to his house and they were glad enough to follow. By Nan's side walked Tige and he licked her hand, just to show that he wanted to make friends with her.

"I guess you are a good dog after all," said she, patting his head. "But you did give me *such* a scare!"

Both of the twins were very cold and glad enough to warm themselves by the kitchen fire while the farmer hitched up his horse. The farmer's wife wished to give them supper, but this they declined, saying they would get supper at home. But she made each eat a big cookie, which tasted exceedingly good.

Soon Farmer Sandborn drove around to the door with his sleigh and in they piled, on the soft straw, with several robes to keep them warm. Then the horse set off on a brisk trot for town.

"It's a nice enough sleigh ride for anybody," declared Bert. And yet they did not enjoy it very much, for fear of what would happen to them when they got home.

"Where in the world have you been?" exclaimed Mrs. Bobbsey as she ran to the door to let them in. "We have been looking all over for you. Your papa was afraid you had been drowned in the lake."

An evening dinner was in waiting for them, and sitting down to satisfy their hunger, they told their story, to which all of the others listened with much interest.

"You can be thankful you weren't blown clear to the other end of the lake," said Mr. Bobbsey. "I think after this you had better leave ice-boating alone."

"I know I shall!" declared Nan.

"Oh, I'll be more careful, papa, after this," pleaded Bert. "You know I promised to go out again with Charley."

"Well then, don't go when the wind is strong," and Bert promised.

"I'm so glad the dog didn't bite you," said little Flossie. "He might have given you hy—hy*dro*pics."

"Flossie means hydrophobics," put in Freddie. "Ain't no hy*dro*pics, is there, Bert?"

"Oh, Freddie, you mean hydrophobia!" burst out Nan, with a laugh.

"No, I mean hydrophobics," insisted the little fellow. "That's what Dinah calls them anyway."

After the adventure on the ice boat matters ran smoothly with the Bobbsey twins for two weeks and more. There was a great deal of snow and as a consequence Freddie and Flossie stayed home from school most of the time. Nan and Bert also remained home two separate days, and during those days all of the children had great fun in the attic, where there was a large storeroom, filled with all sort of things.

"Let us play theater," said Nan, who had been to several exhibitions while at home and while visiting.

"All right," said Bert, falling in with the plan at once. "Let us play Rip Van Winkle. I can be Rip and you can be the loving wife, and Flossie and Freddie can be the children."

Across the storeroom a rope was placed and on this they hung a sliding curtain, made out of a discarded blanket. Then at one side they arranged chairs, and Nan and Flossie brought out their dolls to be the audience.

"They won't clap their hands very much," said Bert. "But then they won't make any disturbance either."

The performance was a great success. It was their own version of Rip Van Winkle, and Bert as old Rip did many funny things which caused Freddie and Flossie to roar with laughter. Nan as the loving wife recited a piece called "Doughnuts and Daisies," pretending to be working around the kitchen in the meantime. The climax was reached when Bert tried to imitate a thunderstorm in the mountains and pulled over a big trunk full of old clothes and some window screens standing in a corner. The show broke up in a hurry, and when Mrs. Bobbsey appeared on the scene, wanting to know what the noise meant, all the actors and the doll audience were out of sight.

But later, when mamma went below again, Bert and Nan sneaked back, and put both the trunk and the screens in their proper places.

Nan's First Cake-baking

"Let's!" cried Nan.

"Yes, let's!" echoed Flossie.

"I want to help too," put in Freddie, "Want to make a cake all by my own self."

"Freddie can make a little cake while we make a big one," said Bert.

It was on an afternoon just a week before Christmas and Mrs. Bobbsey had gone out to do some shopping. Dinah was also away, on a visit to some relatives, so the children had the house all to themselves.

It was Bert who spoke about cake-making first. Queer that a boy should think of it, wasn't it? But Bert was very fond of cake, and did quite some grumbling when none was to be had.

"It ought to be easy to make a nice big plain cake," said Bert. "I've seen Dinah do it lots of times. She just mixes up her milk and eggs and butter, and sifts in the flour, and there you are."

"Much you know about it!" declared Nan. "If it isn't just put together right, it will be as heavy as lead."

"We might take the recipe out of mamma's cook-book," went on Bert; and then the cry went up with which I have opened this chapter.

The twins were soon in the kitchen, which Dinah had left spotlessly clean and in perfect order.

"We mustn't make a muss," warned Nan. "If we do, Dinah will never forgive us."

"As if we couldn't clean it up again," said Bert loftily.

Over the kitchen table they spread some old newspapers, and then Nan brought forth the big bowl in which her mother or the cook usually mixed the cake batter.

"Bert, you get the milk and sugar," said Nan, and began to roll up her sleeves. "Flossie, you can get the butter."

She would have told Freddie to get something, too—just to start them all to work—but Freddie was out of sight.

He had gone into the pantry, where the flour barrel stood. He did not know that Nan intended to use the prepared flour, which was on the shelf. The door worked on a spring, so it closed behind him, shutting him out from the sight of the others.

Taking off the cover of the barrel, Freddie looked inside. The barrel was almost empty, only a few inches of flour remaining at the bottom. There was a flour scoop in the barrel, but he could reach neither this nor the flour itself.

"I'll have to stand on the bench," he said to himself and pulled the bench into position. Then he stood on it and bent down into the barrel as far as possible.

The others were working in the kitchen when they heard a strange *thump* and then a spluttering yell.

"It's Freddie," said Nan. "Bert, go and see what he is doing in the pantry."

Bert ran to the pantry door and pulled it open. A strange sight met his gaze. Out of the top of the barred stuck Freddie's legs, with a cloud of flour dust rising around them. From the bottom of the barrel came a succession of coughs, sneezes, and yells for help.

"Freddie has fallen into the flour barrel!" he cried, and lost no time in catching his brother by the feet and pulling him out. It was hard work and in the midst of it the flour barrel fell over on its side, scattering the flour over the pantry and partly on the kitchen floor.

"Oh! oh! oh!" roared Freddie as soon as he could catch his breath. "Oh, my! oh, my!"

"Oh, Freddie, why did you go into the barrel?" exclaimed Nan, wiping off her hands and running to him. "Did you ever see such a sight before?"

Freddie was digging at the flour in his eyes. He was white from head to feet, and coughing and spluttering.

"Wait, I'll get the whisk-broom," said Bert, and ran for it.

"Brush off his hair first, and then I'll wipe his face," came from Nan.

"Here's the wash-rag," put in little Flossie, and catching it up, wringing wet, she began to wipe off Freddie's face before anybody could stop her.

"Flossie! Flossie! You mustn't do that!" said Bert. "Don't you see you are making paste of the flour?"

The wet flour speedily became a dough on Freddie's face and neck, and he yelled louder than ever. The wash-rag was put away, and regardless of her own clean clothes, Flossie started in to scrape the dough off, until both Nan and Bert made her stop.

"I'll dust him good first," said Bert, and began such a vigorous use of the whisk-broom that everybody began to sneeze.

"Oh, Bert, not so hard!" said Nan, and ran to open the back door. "Bring him here."

Poor Freddie had a lump of dough in his left ear and was trying in vain to get it out with one hand while rubbing his eyes with the other. Nan brushed his face with care, and even wiped off the end of his tongue, and got the lump out of his ear. In the meantime Flossie started to set the flour barrel up once more.

"Don't touch the barrel, Flossie!" called Bert. "You keep away, or you'll be as dirty as Freddie."

It was very hard work to get Freddie's clothes even half clean, and some of the flour refused to budge from his hair. By the time he was made half presentable once more the kitchen was in a mess from end to end.

"What were you doing near the flour barrel?" asked Nan.

"Going to get flour for the cake."

"But we don't want that kind of flour, Freddie. We want this," and she brought forth the package.

"Dinah uses this," answered the little boy.

"Yes, for bread. But we are not going to make bread. You had better sit down and watch Bert and me work, and you, Flossie, had better do the same."

"Ain't no chairs to sit down on," said Freddie, after a look around. "All full of flour."

"I declare, we forgot to dust the chairs," answered Nan. "Bert, will you clean them?"

Bert did so, and Freddie and Flossie sat down to watch the process of cake-making, being assured that they should have the first slices if the cake was a success.

Nan had watched cake-making many times, so she knew exactly how to go to work. Bert was a good helper, and soon the batter was ready for the oven. The fire had been started up, and now Nan put the batter in the cake tin.

The children waited impatiently while the cake was baking. Nan gave Freddie another cleaning, and Bert cleaned up the pantry and the kitchen floor. The flour had made a dreadful mess and the cleaning process was only half-successful.

"'Most time for that cake to be done, isn't it?" questioned Bert, after a quarter of an hour had passed.

"Not quite," answered Nan.

Presently she opened the oven door and tried the cake by sticking a broom whisp into it. The flour was just a bit sticky and she left the cake in a little longer.

When it came out it certainly looked very nice. The top was a golden brown and had raised beautifully. The cake was about a foot in diameter and Nan was justly proud of it.

"Wished you had put raisins in it," said Freddie. "Raisins are beautiful."

"No, I like plain cake the best," said Bert.

"I like chocolate," came from Flossie.

"And I like layer cake, with currant jelly in between," said Nan. "But I didn't dare to open any jelly without asking mamma."

"Let us surprise her with the cake," said Bert.

"Want cake now," protested Freddie. "Don't want to wait 't all!"

But he was persuaded to wait, and the cake was hidden away in the dining-room closet until the hour for the evening meal.

When Dinah came home she noticed the mussed-up kitchen, but Nan begged of her to keep quiet.

"All right, honey," said the colored cook. "But I know youse been a-bakin'—I kin spell it in de air."

When they sat down to the evening meal all of the children produced the cake in great triumph.

"Oh, Nan, a real cake!" cried Mrs. Bobbsey. "How nice it looks!"

"We've got some real housekeepers around here," said Mr. Bobbsey. "I'll have to try that sure."

When the cake was cut all ate liberally of it. They declared it just right and said it could not be better. Even Dinah was tickled.

"Couldn't do no better maself," she declared. "Bymeby Dinah will be cut out of a job—wid Miss Nan a-doin' ob de bakin'."

"No, Dinah, you shall stay even if I do do the baking," answered Nan; and went to bed feeling very happy.

Christmas

As the time for Christmas drew shorter all of the Bobbsey children wondered what Santa Claus would bring them and what they would receive from their relatives at a distance.

Freddie and Flossie had made out long lists of the things they hoped to get. Freddie wished a fireman's suit with a real trumpet, a railroad track with a locomotive that could go, and some building blocks and picture books. Flossie craved more dolls and dolls' dresses, a real trunk with a lock, fancy slippers, a pair of rubber boots, and some big card games.

"All I want is a set of furs," said Nan, not once but many times. "A beautiful brown set, just like mamma's."

"And all I want is some good story books, some games, a new pocket-knife, a big wagon, and some money," said Bert.

"Mercy, you don't want much, Bert," cried Nan. "How much money—a thousand dollars?"

"I want money, too," piped in Freddie. "Want to start a bank account just like papa's."

By dint of hard saving Bert and Nan had accumulated two dollars and ten cents between them, while Freddie and Flossie had each thirty-five cents. There was a wonderful lot of planning between the twins, and all put their money together, to buy papa and mamma and Dinah and Sam some Christmas presents. Freddie and Flossie had not yet purchased the cologne and handkerchief before mentioned, and now it was decided to get Mr. Bobbsey a new cravat, Mrs. Bobbsey a flower in a pot, Dinah a fancy apron, and Sam a pair of gloves. Nan and Bert made the purchases which, after being duly inspected by all, were hidden away in the garret storeroom.

As the time for Christmas came on Flossie and Freddie grew very anxious, wanting to know if Santa Claus would be sure to come. Flossie inspected the chimney several times.

"It's a dreadfully small place and very dirty," said she. "I am afraid Santa Claus won't be able to get down with a very big load. And some of his things will get all mussed up."

"Santa Claus can spirit himself wherever he wants to, dear," said Mrs. Bobbsey, with a quiet smile.

"What do you mean by *spirit* himself, mamma?"

"Never mind now, Flossie; you'll understand that when you grow older."

"Does mamma mean a ghost?" asked Flossie, later on, of Nan.

"No, Flossie; she means the part of a person that lives but can't be seen."

"Oh, I know," cried the child, brightening. "It's just like when a person is good. Then they say it's the *spirit* of goodness within him. I guess it's the good spirit of Santa Claus that can't be seen. But we can feel it, can't we? and that's what's best."

On the day before Christmas the sitting-room door was closed and locked, so that none of the children might enter the room. Freddie was very anxious to look through the keyhole, but Bert told him that wouldn't be fair, so he stayed away.

"We are to hang up our stockings to-night," said Nan. "And mamma says we must go to bed early, too."

"That's to give Santa Claus a chance to get around," said Freddie. "Papa said so. He said Santa Claus had his hands more than full, with so many boys and girls all over the world to take care of."

"Santa Claus must be a twin, just like you and me," said Flossie. "Maybe he's a twin a hundred times over."

At this Freddie roared. "What a funny twin that would be—with each one having the same name!"

The stockings were hung up with great care, and Freddie and Flossie made up their minds to stay awake and watch Santa Claus at his work.

"Won't say a word when he comes," said the little boy. "Just peek out at him from under the covers." But alas! long before Santa Claus paid his visit that Christmas Eve both Freddie and Flossie were in dreamland, and so were Bert and Nan.

It was Flossie who was the first awake in the morning. For the moment after she opened her eyes and sat up she could not remember why she had awakened thus early. But it was for some reason, she was sure of that.

"Merry Christmas!" she burst out, all at once, and the cry awoke Freddie. "Merry Christmas!" he repeated. "Merry Christmas, ev'rybody!" he roared out, at the top of his lungs.

The last call awoke Nan and Bert, and before long all were scrambling out to see what the stockings might contain.

"Oh, I've got a doll!" shrieked Flossie, and brought forth a wonderful affair of paper.

"I have a jumping-jack!" came from Freddie, and he began to work the toy up and down in a most comical fashion.

There was some small gift for everybody and several apples and oranges besides, and quantities of nuts in the stockings.

"We must get the presents for the others," whispered Nan to Bert and the smaller twins, and soon all were dressed and bringing the things down from the storeroom.

It was a happy party that gathered in the dining room. "Merry Christmas!" said everybody to everybody else, and then Mr. Bobbsey, who was in the sitting room, blew a horn and opened the folding doors.

There, on a large side stand, rested a beautiful Christmas tree, loaded down with pretty ornaments and apples and candies, and with many prettily colored candles. Around the bottom of the tree were four heaps of presents, one for each of the children.

"Oh, look at the big doll!" screamed Flossie, and caught the present up in her arms and kissed it.

"And look at my fireman's suit!" roared Freddie, and then, seeing a trumpet, he took it up and bellowed: "Bring up the engine! Play away lively there!" just like a real fireman.

Bert had his books and other things, and under them was hidden a real bank book, showing that there had been deposited to his credit ten dollars in the Lakeport Savings Bank. Nan had a similar bank book, and of these the twins were very, very proud. Bert felt as if he was truly getting to be quite a business man.

"Oh! oh!" cried Nan, as she opened a big box that was at the bottom of her pile of presents, and then the tears of joy stood in her eyes as she brought forth the hoped-for set of furs. They were beautiful, and so soft she could not resist brushing them against her cheek over and over again.

"Oh, mamma, I think they are too lovely for anything!" she said, rushing up and kissing her parent. "I am sure no girl ever had such a nice set of furs before!"

"You must try to keep them nice, Nan," answered the mother.

"I shall take the very best of care of them," said Nan, and my readers may be sure that she did.

"And now we have something for you, too," said Bert, and brought out the various articles. Flossie gave their mamma her present, and Freddie gave papa what was coming to him. Then Nan gave Dinah the fancy apron and Bert took Sam the new gloves.

"Well this is truly a surprise!" cried Mr. Bobbsey, as he inspected the cravat. "It is just what I need."

"And this flower is beautiful," said Mrs. Bobbsey as she smelt of the potted plant. "It will bloom a long while, I am sure."

Dinah was tickled over the apron and Sam with his gloves.

"Yo' chillun am the sweetest in de world," said the cook.

"Dem globes am de werry t'ing I needed to keep ma hands warm," came from Sam.

It was fully an hour before the children felt like sitting down to breakfast. Before they began the repast Mr. Bobbsey brought forth the family Bible and read the wonderful story of Christ's birth to them, and asked the blessing. All were almost too excited to eat.

After breakfast all must go out and show their presents to their friends and see what the friends had received. It was truly a happy time. Then all went coasting until lunch.

"The expressman is coming!" cried Bert a little later, and sure enough he drove up to the Bobbsey house with two boxes. One was from their Uncle Daniel Bobbsey, who lived at Meadow Brook, and the other from their Uncle William Minturn, who lived at Ocean Cliff.

"More presents!" cried Nan, and she was right. Uncles and aunts had sent each something; and the twins were made happier than ever.

"Oh, but Christmas is just the best day in the whole year," said Bert that evening, after the eventful day was over.

"Wish Christmas would come ev'ry week," said Freddie. "Wouldn't it be *beau*tiful?"

"If it did I'm afraid the presents wouldn't reach," said Mrs. Bobbsey, and then took him and Flossie off to bed.

The Children's Party

The little black kitten that Freddie had brought home from the department store was a great friend to everybody in the Bobbsey house and all loved the little creature very much.

At first Freddie started to call the kitten Blackie, but Flossie said that wasn't a very "'ristocratic" name at all.

"I'll tell you what," said Bert jokingly, "Let's call him Snoop," and in spite of all efforts to make the name something else Snoop the cat remained from that time to the day of his death.

He grew very fat and just a trifle lazy, nevertheless he learned to do several tricks. He could sit up in a corner on his hind legs, and shake hands, and when told to do so would jump through one's arms, even if the arms were quite high up from the floor.

Snoop had one comical trick that always made both Flossie and Freddie laugh. There was running water in the kitchen, and Snoop loved to sit on the edge of the sink and play with the drops as they fell from the bottom of the faucet. He would watch until a drop was just falling, then reach out with his paw and give it a claw just as if he was reaching for a mouse.

Another trick he had, but this Mrs. Bobbsey did not think so nice, was to curl himself on the pillow of one of the beds and go sound asleep. Whenever he heard Mrs. Bobbsey coming up one pair of stairs, he would fly off the bed and sneak down the other pair, so that she caught him but rarely.

Snoop was a very clean cat and was continually washing his face and his ears. Around his neck Flossie placed a blue ribbon, and it was amusing to see Snoop try to wash it off. But after a while, having spoilt several ribbons, he found they would not wash off, and so he let them alone, and in the end appeared very proud of them.

One day, when Snoop had been in the house but a few months, he could not be found anywhere.

"Snoop! Snoop!" called Freddie, upstairs and down, but the kitten did not answer, nor did he show himself. Then Flossie called him and made a search, but was equally unsuccessful.

"Perhaps somebody has stolen him," said Freddie soberly.

"Nobody been heah to steal dat kitten," answered Dinah. "He's jess sneaked off, dat's all."

All of the children had been invited to a party that afternoon and Nan was going to wear her new set of furs. After having her hair brushed, and putting on a white dress, Nan went to the closet in which her furs were kept in the big box.

"Well, I never!" she ejaculated. "Oh, Snoop! however could you do it!"

For there, curled up on the set of furs, was the kitten, purring as contentedly as could be. Never before had he found a bed so soft or so to his liking. But Nan made him rouse up in a hurry, and after that when she closed the closet she made quite sure that Snoop was not inside.

The party to be held that afternoon was at the home of Grace Lavine, the little girl who had fainted from so much rope jumping. Grace was over that attack, and was now quite certain that when her mamma told her to do a thing or to leave it alone, it was always for her own good.

"Mamma knows best," she said to Nan. "I didn't think so then, but I do now."

The party was a grand affair and over thirty young people were present, all dressed in their best. They played all sorts of games such as many of my readers must already know, and then some new games which the big boys and girls introduced.

One game was called Hunt the Beans. A handful of dried beans was hidden all over the rooms, in out-of-the-way corners, behind the piano, in vases, and like that, and at the signal to start every girl and boy started to pick up as many as could be found. The search lasted just five minutes, and at the end of that time the one having the most beans won the game.

"Now let us play Three-word Letters," said Nan. And then she explained the game. "I will call out a letter and you must try to think of a sentence of three words, each word starting with that letter. Now then, are you ready?"

"Yes! yes!" the girls and boys cried.

"B," said Nan.

There was a second of silence.

"Boston Baked Beans!" shouted Charley Mason.

"That is right, Charley. Now it is your turn to give a letter."

"F," said Charley.

"Five Fat Fairies!" cried Nellie Parks.

"Four Fresh Fish," put in another of the girls.

"Nellie has it," said Charley. "But I never heard of fat fairies, did you?" and this question made everybody laugh.

"My letter is M," said Nellie, after a pause.

"More Minced Mushrooms," said Bert.

"More Mean Men," said another boy.

"Mind My Mule," said one of the girls.

"Oh, Helen, I didn't know you had a mule," cried Flossie, and this caused a wild shriek of laughter.

"Bert must love mushrooms," said Nellie.

"I do," said Bert, "if they are in a sauce." And then the game went on, until somebody suggested something else.

At seven o'clock a supper was served. The tables were two in number, with the little girls and boys at one and the big girls and boys at the other. Each was decked out with flowers and with colored streamers, which ran down from the chandelier to each corner of both tables.

There was a host of good things to eat and drink—chicken sandwiches and cake, with cups of sweet chocolate, or lemonade, and then more cake and ice-cream, and fruit, nuts, and candy. The ice-cream was done up into various fancy forms, and Freddie got a fireman, with a trumpet under his arm, and Nan a Japanese lady with a real paper parasol over her head. Bert was served with an automobile, and Flossie cried with delight when she received a brown-and-white cow that looked as natural as life. All of the forms were so pleasing that the children did not care to eat them until the heat in the lighted dining room made them begin to melt away.

"I'm going to tell Dinah about the ice-cream cow," said Flossie. "Perhaps she can make them." But when appealed to, the cook said they were beyond her, and must be purchased from the professional ice-cream maker, who had the necessary forms.

There were dishes full of bonbons on the tables, and soon the bonbons were snapping at a lively rate among the big girls and boys, although the younger folks were rather afraid of them. Each bonbon had a motto paper in it and some sort of fancy article made of paper. Bert got an apron, which he promptly pinned on, much to the amusement of the girls. Nan drew a workman's cap and put it on, and this caused another laugh. There were all sorts of caps, hats, and aprons, and one big bonbon, which went to Flossie, had a complete dress in it, of pink and white paper. Another had some artificial flowers, and still another a tiny bottle of cologne.

While the supper was going on, Mr. Lavine had darkened the parlor and stretched a sheet over the folding doors, and as soon as the young people were through eating they were treated to a magic-lantern exhibition by the gentleman of the house and one of the big boys, who assisted him. There were all sorts of scenes, including some which were very funny and made the boys and girls shriek with laughter. One was a boy on a donkey, and another two fat men trying to climb over a fence. Then came a number of pictures made from photograph negatives, showing scenes in and around Lakeport. There were the lake steamer, and the main street, and one picture of the girls and boys rushing out of school at dinner time. The last was voted the best of all, and many present tried to pick themselves out of this picture and did so.

After the exhibition was over one of the largest of the girls sat down to the piano and played. By this time some of the older folks drifted in, and they called for some singing, and all joined in half a dozen songs that were familiar to them. Then the young folks ran off for their coats and caps and wraps, and bid their host and hostess and each other good-night.

"Wasn't it splendid?" said Nan, on the way home. "I never had such a good time before."

"Didn't last half long enough," said Freddie. "Want it to last longer next time."

"I wanted my cow to last longer," said Flossie. "Oh, if only I could have kept it from melting!"

A Grand Sleigh Ride

For a long while all of the Bobbsey children had been begging their parents for a sleigh ride into the country.

"The winter will be gone soon, papa," said Nan. "Won't you take us before the snow is all gone?"

"You may as well take them, Richard," said Mrs. Bobbsey.

"Well, if I do, Mary, you must go along," answered Mr. Bobbsey, and so it was arranged that they should take the ride on the following Saturday, weather permitting.

You may well suppose that all of the twins were very anxious about the weather after that, for Mr. Bobbsey said he would not go if it rained or if it snowed very hard.

"What does it say in the newspapers?" asked Freddie. "They always know what the weather is going to be."

"Not so far ahead as that," answered his brother.

But Friday evening the paper said cold and clear, and sure enough, on Saturday morning it was as nice as one would wish. From behind masses of thin clouds the sun peeped shyly, lighting up the snow until it shone like huge beds of diamonds.

They were to drive to Dalton, twelve miles away. Mr. Bobbsey had learned that the road to Dalton was in good condition, and the family had friends there who would be pleased to see them and have them remain to dinner.

By half-past nine the big family sleigh was at the door, with Sam on the front seat, driving. Into the sleigh piled the four children, and Mr. and Mrs. Bobbsey followed.

"Want to sit by Sam and help drive," said Freddie, and he was lifted over to the desired position. Then off they went, with a crack of the whip and jingling of sleigh-bells that could be heard a long distance.

"Oh, but isn't this just too splendid for anything!" exclaimed Nan, who sat at one side of the seat, with her mamma on the other and Flossie between them. "I do love sleigh riding so much!"

"See me drive!" cried Freddie, who held the very end of the reins, the part dangling from Sam's hands.

"Well, Freddie, don't let the team run away," said Mr. Bobbsey, with a laugh.

"I shan't," answered the little fellow soberly. "If they try to run away, I'll whip them good."

"You'll never stop them that way," said Bert. "You want to talk gently to them."

On and on they went, over the smooth snow. The horses were fresh and full of spirit, and mile after mile was passed with a speed that pleased all of the twins very much. They passed several other sleighing parties, and every time this was done the children set up a merry shout which was sure to call forth an equally merry answer.

A large part of the ride was through the country, and often the country folks would come to the doors to see them pass. Once they met a boy on the road and he asked for a ride to his home, half a mile away.

"Yes, jump in," said Mr. Bobbsey, and the boy got in and was taken to his house almost before he knew it.

"Much obliged," he said on leaving them. "You're fine people, you are," and he took off his hat at parting.

"It was nice to give him a ride," said Nan. "It didn't cost us anything and he liked it a great deal, I am sure."

"We must never forget to do a kindness when we can, Nan," said her mamma.

Before noon Dalton was reached and they drove up to the home of Mr. Ramdell, as their friend was named. Immediately Bob Ramdell, a youth of sixteen, rushed eagerly out to greet Bert.

"I'm glad you've come," he cried. "I've been watching for you for an hour."

"It isn't noon yet," answered Bert.

All were soon into the house and Sam drove the sleigh around to the barn. Bob Ramdell had a sister Susie, who was almost Nan's age, and a baby brother called Tootsie, although his real name was Alexander. Susie was glad to see Nan and Flossie, and all were soon playing with the baby, who was just old enough to be amusing.

"I've got a plan on hand," whispered Bob to Bert, just before dinner was served. "I've been wondering if your father will let us carry it out."

"What is it?" questioned Bert.

"You are not to drive home until late this afternoon. I wonder if your father won't let you go down to Long Lake with me after dinner, to see the hockey match."

"Is it far from here?"

"About two miles. We can drive down in our cutter. Father will let me have the cutter and old Rusher, I'm sure."

"I'll see about it," said Bert. "I'd like to see the hockey match very much."

As soon as he got the chance Bert questioned his parent about going.

"I don't know about this," said Mr. Bobbsey slowly. "Do you think you two boys can be trusted alone with the horse?"

"Oh, yes, papa. Bob has driven old Rusher many times."

"You must remember, Rusher used to be a race horse. He may run away with Bob and you."

"Oh, but that was years ago, papa. He is too old to run away now. Please say yes."

Bert continued to plead, and in the end Mr. Bobbsey gave him permission to go to the hockey match.

"But you must be back before five o'clock," said he. "We are going to start for home at that time."

The dinner was a fine one and tasted especially good to the children after their long ride. But Bert and Bob were impatient to be off, and left the moment they had disposed of their pieces of pie.

Old Rusher was a black steed which, in years gone by, had won many a race on the track. He had belonged to a brother to Mr. Ramdell, who had died rather suddenly two years before. He was, as Bert had said, rather old, but there was still a good deal of fire left in him, as the boys were soon to discover to their cost.

The road to Long Lake was a winding one, up one hill and down another, and around a sharp turn where in years gone by there had been a sand pit.

In the best of spirits the two boys started off, Bob handling the reins like a veteran driver. Bob loved horses, and his one ambition in life was to handle a "spanking team," as he called it.

"Old Rusher can go yet," said Bert, who enjoyed the manner in which the black steed stepped out. "He must have been a famous race horse in his day."

"He was," answered Bob. "He won ever so many prizes."

The distance to Long Lake was covered almost before Bert knew it. As the hockey game was not yet begun they spent half an hour in driving over the road that led around the lake.

Quite a crowd had gathered, some in sleighs and some on foot, and the surface of the lake was covered with skaters. When the hockey game started the crowd watched every move with interest.

It was a "hot" game, according to Bert, and when a clever play was made he applauded as loudly as the rest. When the game was at an end he was sorry to discover that it was after four o'clock.

"We must get home," said he to Bob. "I promised to be back by five."

"Oh, we'll get back in no time," said Bob. "Remember, Rusher has had a good rest."

They were soon on the road again, Rusher kicking up his heels livelier than before, for the run down to the lake had merely enabled him to get the stiffness out of his limbs.

Sleighs were on all sides and, as the two boys drove along, two different sleighing parties passed them.

"Hullo, Ramdell!" shouted a young man in a cutter. "Got out old Rusher, I see. Want a race?"

"I think I can beat you!" shouted back Bob, and in a moment more the two cutters were side by side, and each horse and driver doing his best to win.

"Oh, Bob, can you hold him?" cried Bert.

"To be sure I can!" answered Bob. "Just you let me alone and see."

"Come on!" yelled the stranger. "Come on, or I'll leave you behind in no time!"

"You'll not leave me behind so quickly," answered Bob. "Go it, Rusher, go it!" he added to his horse, and the steed flew over the smooth road at a rate of speed that filled Bert with astonishment.

The Race and the Runaway

Bert loved to ride and drive, but it must be confessed that he did not enjoy racing.

The road was rather uneven, and he could not help but think what the consequences might be if the cutter should strike a deep hollow or a big stone.

"Don't let Rusher run away," he said to his friend. "Be careful."

Bob was by this time having his hands so full that he could not answer.

"Steady, Rusher, steady!" he called out to the steed. "Steady, old boy!"

But the old race horse was now warmed up to his work and paid no attention to what was said. On and on he sped, until the young man in the other cutter was gradually outdistanced.

"Told you I could beat you!" flung back Bob.

"The race is yours," answered the young man, in much disappointment, and then he dropped further back than ever.

"Better slacken up, Bob," said Bert. "There is no use in driving so hard now."

"I—I can't slacken up," answered Bob. "Steady, Rusher," he called out. "Whoa, old fellow, whoa!"

But the old race horse did not intend to whoa, and on he flew as fast as his legs would carry him, up the first hill and then onward toward the turn before mentioned.

"Be careful at the turn, Bob!" screamed Bert. "Be careful, or we'll go over!"

"Whoa, Rusher!" repeated Bob, and pulled in on the reins with all of his might.

The turn where the sand pit had been was now close at hand. Here the road was rather narrow, so they had to drive close to the opening, now more than half filled with drifted snow. Bert clung to the cutter while Bob continued to haul in on the reins. Then came a crash, as the cutter hit a hidden stone and drove straight for the sand pit.

"Hold on!" cried Bob, and the next instant Bert found himself flying out of the cutter and over the edge of the road. He tried to save himself by clutching at the ice and snow, but it was useless, and in a twinkling he disappeared into the sand pit! Bob followed, while Rusher went on more gayly than ever, hauling the overturned cutter after him.

Down and down went poor Bert into the deep snow, until he thought he was never going to stop. Bob was beside him, and both floundered around wildly until almost the bottom of the pit was reached.

"Oh, Bob!"

"Oh, Bert! Are you hurt?"

"Don't know as I am. But what a tumble!"

"Rusher has run away!"

"I was afraid he'd do that."

For a minute the two boys knew not what to do. The deep snow lay all around them and how to get out of the pit was a serious question.

"It's a wonder we weren't smothered," said Bob. "Are you quite sure no bones have been broken?"

"Bones broken? Why, Bob, it was like coming down on a big feather bed. I only hope Rusher doesn't do any damage."

"So do I."

When the boys finally floundered out of the hollow into which they had fallen, they found themselves in snow up to their waists. On all sides of them were the walls of the sand pit, ten to fifteen feet high.

"I don't see how we are going to get out of this," said Bert dolefully. "We can't climb out."

"We'll have to do it," answered Bob. "Come, follow me."

He led the way through the deep snow to where the walls did not seem to be so high. At one spot the rain had washed down part of the soil.

"Let us try to climb up that slope," said the larger boy and led the way, and Bert followed.

It was hard work and it made Bert pant for breath, for the snow was still up to his waist. But both kept on, and in the end they stood on the edge of the sand pit, opposite to the side which ran along the road.

"Now we have got to walk around," said Bob. "But that will be easy, if we keep to the places where the wind has swept the snow away."

At last they stood on the road, and this reached both struck out for Dalton, less than a mile away.

"I'm afraid I'll catch it, if Rusher has smashed up the cutter," said Bob as they hurried along.

"We did wrong to race," answered Bert.

"Humph! it's no use to cry over spilt milk, Bert."

"I know that, Bob. Was the cutter a new one?"

"No, but I know father won't want it smashed up."

Much downhearted the boys kept on walking. Bert had not wanted to race, yet he felt he was guilty for having taken part. Perhaps his father would have to pay for part of the damage done.

"Maybe old Rusher ran right into town and smashed things right and left," he said to his friend.

"It would be just like him," sighed Bob. "It will make an awful bill to pay, won't it?"

A little further on they came to where a barn and a wagon shed lined the road. Under the shed stood a horse and cutter.

"My gracious me!" burst out Bob.

"Why—why—is it Rusher?" gasped Bert.

"It is!" shouted his friend.

Both boys ran up, and as they did so a farmer came from the barn.

"Oh, Mr. Daly, did you catch our horse?"

"I did, Bob," said the farmer. "Had a runaway, eh?"

"Yes, sir. Rusher threw us both into the old sand pit. I'm ever so glad you caught him. Is the cutter broken?"

"Not that I noticed. I knew you must have had a spill-out. I saw you going to the lake right after dinner."

Both boys inspected the cutter and found it in good condition, outside of a few scratches that did not count. Old Rusher was also all right, for which they were thankful.

"It was nice of you to stop the horse," said Bert to Farmer Daly.

"Oh, I'd do as much for anybody," said the farmer. "That is, if it wasn't too dangerous. Rusher wasn't running very fast when I caught him."

"He was running fast enough when he threw us out," answered Bob.

It did not take the boys long to get into the cutter again.

"Don't let him get away on the road home," sang out Farmer Daly after them.

"No fear of that," answered Bob.

He was very careful how he let Rusher step out. It was growing late, but Bert did not urge him on, so it was half-past five before the Ramdell house was reached.

"You are late after all," said Mr. Bobbsey, rather displeased.

"Oh, we've had such an adventure," cried Bert.

"What happened to you?" questioned Mrs. Bobbsey quickly.

"Rusher threw us into a sand pit," answered Bert, and then told the whole story.

"You can be thankful that you were not hurt," said his mamma.

"I am thankful, mamma."

"Rusher is still full of go," said Mrs. Ramdell. "I have warned my husband not to let Bob drive him."

"Oh, it was the brush with the other cutter that did it," said Bob. "Rusher couldn't stand it to let another horse pass him on the road."

Shortly after this, good-bys were said, and Sam brought around the big family sleigh from the barn. Into this the whole Bobbsey family piled, and off they went, in the gathering gloom of the short winter day.

"I've had a lovely time!" called out Nan.

"So have I had a lovely time," added little Flossie.

"Splendid," came from Freddie. "The baby is awful nice to play with."

"I've had a good time, too," said Bert. "The hockey game was just the best ever, and so was the drive behind Rusher, even if we did get dumped out."

The drive back to Lakeport was enjoyed as much as the drive to Dalton in the morning. On the way the children began to sing, and the voices mingled sweetly with the sounds of the sleigh bells.

"I shall not forget this outing in a hurry," said Nan, as she leaped to the step and ran into the house.

"I shan't forget it either," answered Bert. "But it turned out differently for me from what I thought it would."

A Quarrel in the Schoolyard

Three days after the grand sleighing party to Dalton, Nan came down to breakfast looking very pale and worried.

"What is the trouble, Nan?" questioned her mamma. "What has happened?"

"Oh, mamma, I scarcely feel like telling," answered Nan. "I am afraid you'll laugh at me."

"I fancy you had best tell me," went on Mrs. Bobbsey.

"I saw the ghost last night—or rather, early this morning."

"What, the ghost that I saw?" shouted Bert.

"I think it must have been the same. Anyway, it was about that high"—Nan raised her hand to her shoulder—"and all pure white."

"Oh, Nan!" shivered Freddie. "Don't want no ghostses!"

"I don't want to see it," put in Flossie, and edged closer to her mamma as if fearful the ghost might walk into the dining room that minute.

"This is certainly strange," came from Mr. Bobbsey. "Tell us all about it, Nan."

"Oh, papa, you won't laugh?" and Nan's face grew very red. "I—I—didn't think of it then, but it must have been very funny," she continued.

"It's not very funny to see a ghost, Nan," said Mrs. Bobbsey.

"I don't mean that—I mean what I did afterward. You see I was asleep and I woke up all of a sudden, for I thought somebody had passed a hand over my face. When I looked out into the room the ghost was standing right in front of the dresser. I could see into the glass and for the minute I thought there were two ghosts."

"Oh!" came from Flossie. "Two! Wasn't that simply dreadful!" And she crouched closer than ever to her mamma.

"As I was looking, the ghost moved away toward the window and then I saw there was but one. I was so scared I couldn't call anybody."

"I believe you," said Bert. "It's awful, isn't it?"

"This is certainly strange," said Mr. Bobbsey, with a grave look on his face. "What did you do next, Nan."

"You—you won't laugh, papa?"

"No."

"I thought of my umbrella. It was resting against the wall, close to the bed. I turned over and reached for the umbrella, but it slipped down and made a terrible noise as it struck the floor. Then I flung the covers over my head."

"What did you want the umbrella for?" questioned Freddie, in great wonder. "'Twasn't raining."

"I thought I could—could punch the ghost with it," faltered Nan.

At this Bert could hold in no longer, and he set up a shout of laughter, which was instantly repressed by Mr. Bobbsey.

"Oh, Nan, I'm sorry I laughed," said her twin brother, when he could speak. "But the idea of your poking at a ghost with an umbrella!"

"It was more than you tried to do," said Mr. Bobbsey dryly.

"That is so." Bert grew red in the face. "Did you see the ghost after that?" he asked to hide his confusion.

"No."

"Not at all?" asked Mrs. Bobbsey.

"No, mamma. I stayed under the covers for about a minute—just like Bert did—and when I looked the ghost was gone."

"I will have to investigate this," said Mr. Bobbsey seriously. "It is queer that neither I nor your mamma has seen the ghost."

"I ain't seen it," said Flossie.

"Don't want to see it," piped in Freddie.

Dinah, in the kitchen, had heard Nan's story and she was almost scared to death.

"Dat am de strangest t'ing," she said to Sam, when he came for his dinner. "Wot yo' make of it, hey?"

"Dunno," said Sam. "Maybe sumbuddy's gwine to die."

The matter was talked over by the Bobbsey family several times that day, and Mr. Bobbsey remained awake nearly all of that night, on the watch for the ghost. The following night Mrs. Bobbsey watched, and then Dinah took her turn, followed by Sam, who sat in the upper hall in a rocking chair, armed with a club. But the ghost failed to show itself, and after a week the excitement died down once more.

"Perhaps you were dreaming, Nan," said Mrs. Bobbsey.

"No, I wasn't dreaming, mamma, and Bert says he wasn't dreaming either."

"It is strange. I cannot understand it at all."

"Do you believe in ghosts, mamma?"

"No, my dear."

"But I saw something."

"Perhaps it was only a reflection. Sometimes the street lamps throw strange shadows on the walls through the windows."

"It wasn't a shadow," said Nan; and there the talk ended, for Mrs. Bobbsey knew not what to say to comfort her daughter.

In some way the news that a ghost had been seen in the Bobbsey house spread throughout the neighborhood, and many came to ask about it. Even the boys and girls talked about it and asked Nan and Bert all manner of questions, the most of which the twins could not answer.

The "ghost talk," as it was called, gave Danny Rugg a good chance to annoy both Nan and Bert.

"Afraid of a ghost! Afraid of a ghost!" he would cry, whenever he saw them. "Oh, my, but ain't I afraid of a ghost!"

"I think it is perfectly dreadful," said Nan one day, on returning from school. Her eyes were red, showing that she had been crying.

"I'll 'ghost' him, if he yells at us again," said Bert. "I'm not going to stand it, so there!"

"But what will you do, Bert?"

"I'll fight him, that's what I'll do."

"Oh, Bert, you mustn't fight."

"Then he has got to leave you alone—and leave me alone, too."

"If you fight at school, you'll be expelled."

"I don't care, I'm going to make him mind his own business," said Bert recklessly.

Danny Rugg was particularly sore because he had not been invited to Grace Lavine's party. Of all the boys in that neighborhood he was the only one left out, and he fancied it was Nan and Bert's fault.

"They don't like me and they are setting everybody against me," he thought. "I shan't stand it, not me!"

Two days later he followed Bert into the schoolyard, in which a large number of boys were playing.

"Hullo! how's the ghost?" he cried. "Is it still living at your house?"

"You be still about that ghost, Danny Rugg!" cried Bert, with flashing eyes.

"Oh, but wouldn't I like to have a house with a ghost," went on Danny tantalizingly. "And a sister who was afraid of it!"

"Will you be still, or not?"

"Why should I be still? You've got the ghost, haven't you? And Nan is scared to death of it, isn't she?"

"No, she isn't."

"Yes, she is, and so are you and all the rest of the family." And then Danny set up his old shout: "Afraid of a ghost! Afraid of a ghost!"

Some of the other boys followed suit and soon a dozen or more were crying, "Afraid of a ghost!" as loudly as they could.

Bert grew very pale and his breath came thickly. He watched Danny and when he came closer caught him by the arm.

"Let go!" cried the big boy roughly.

"I want you to stop calling like that."

"I shan't stop."

"I say you will!"

Bert had hardly spoken when Danny struck at him and hit him in the arm. Then Bert struck out in return and hit Danny in the chin. A dozen or more blows followed in quick succession. One struck Bert in the eye and blackened that organ, and another reached Danny's nose and made it bleed. Then the two boys clinched and rolled over on the schoolyard pavement.

"A fight! A fight!" came from those looking on, and this was taken up on all sides, while many crowded forward to see what was going on.

The school principal, Mr. Tetlow, was just entering the school at the time. Hearing the cry he ran around into the yard.

"Boys! boys! what does this mean?" he demanded, and forced his way through the crowd to where Bert and Danny lay, still pummeling each other. "Stand up at once and behave yourselves," and reaching down, he caught each by the collar and dragged him to his feet.

Nan's Plea

Bert's heart sank when he saw that it was the school principal who held him by the collar. He remembered what Nan had said about fighting and being expelled.

"It was Bert Bobbsey's fault," blustered Danny, wiping his bleeding nose on his sleeve.

"No, it wasn't," answered Bert quickly. "It was his fault."

"I say it was your fault!" shouted Danny. "He started the fight, Mr. Tetlow."

"He struck first," went on Bert undauntedly.

"He caught me by the arm and wouldn't let me go," came from Danny.

"I told him to keep still," explained Bert. "He was calling, 'Afraid of a ghost!' at me and I don't like it. And he said my sister Nan was afraid of it, too."

"Both of you march up to my office," said Mr. Tetlow sternly. "And remain there until I come."

"My nose is bleeding," whined Danny.

"You may go and wash your nose first," said the principal.

With a heart that was exceedingly heavy Bert entered the school and made his way to the principal's office. No one was there, and he sank on a chair in a corner. He heard the bells ring and heard the pupils enter the school and go to their various classrooms.

"If I am sent home, what will mamma and papa say?" he thought dismally. He had never yet been sent home for misconduct, and the very idea filled him with nameless dread.

His eye hurt him not a little, but to this he just then paid no attention. He was wondering what Mr. Tetlow would have to say when he came.

Presently the door opened and Danny shuffled in, a wet and bloody handkerchief held to his nose. He sat down on the opposite side of the office, and for several minutes nothing was said by either of the boys.

"I suppose you are going to try to get me into trouble," said Danny at length.

"You're trying to get me into trouble," returned Bert. "I didn't start the quarrel, and you know it."

"I don't know nothing of the kind, Bert Bobbsey! If you say I started the fight—I'll—I'll—tell something more about you."

"Really?"

"Yes, really."

"What can you tell?"

"You know well enough. Mr. Ringley hasn't forgotten about his broken window."

"Well, you broke that, I didn't."

"Humph! maybe I can prove that you broke it."

"Danny Rugg, what do you mean?" exclaimed Bert. "You know I had nothing to do with that broken window."

The big boy was about to say something more in reply when Mr. Tetlow entered the office.

"Boys," said he abruptly, "this is a disgraceful affair. I thought both of you knew better than to fight. It is setting a very bad example to the rest of the scholars. I shall have to punish you both severely."

Mr. Tetlow paused and Bert's heart leaped into his throat. What if he should be expelled? The very thought of it made him shiver.

"I have made a number of inquiries of the other pupils, and I find that you, Danny, started the quarrel. You raised the cry of 'Afraid of a ghost!' when you had no right to do so, and when Bert caught you by the arm and told you to stop you struck him. Is this true?"

"I—I—he hit me in the chin. I told him to let me go."

"He struck me first, Mr. Tetlow," put in Bert. "I am sure all of the boys will say the same."

"Hem! Bert, you can go to your classroom. I will talk to you after school this afternoon."

Somewhat relieved Bert left the office and walked to the classroom, where the other pupils eyed him curiously. It was hard work to put his mind on his lessons, but he did his best, for he did not wish to miss in any of them and thus make matters worse.

"What did the principal do?" whispered the boy who sat next to him.

"Hasn't done anything yet," whispered Bert in return.

"It was Danny's fault," went on the boy. "We'll stick by you."

At noontime Bert walked home with Nan, feeling very much downcast.

"Oh, Bert, what made you fight?" said his twin sister. "I told you not to."

"I couldn't help it, Nan. He told everybody that you were afraid of the ghost."

"And what is Mr. Tetlow going to do?"

"I don't know. He told me to stay in after school this afternoon, as he wanted to talk with me."

"If he expels you, mamma will never get over it."

"I know that, Nan. But—but—I couldn't stand it to have him yelling out, 'Afraid of a ghost!'"

After that Nan said but little. But her thoughts were busy, and by the time they were returning to the school her mind was fully made up.

To all of the school children the principal's office was a place that usually filled them with awe. Rarely did anybody go there excepting when sent by a teacher because of some infringements of the rules.

Nan went to school early that afternoon, and as soon as she had left Bert and the two younger twins, she marched bravely to Mr. Tetlow's office and knocked on the door.

"Come in," said the principal, who was at his desk looking over some school reports.

"If you please, Mr. Tetlow, I came to see you about my brother, Bert Bobbsey," began Nan.

Mr. Tetlow looked at her kindly, for he half expected what was coming.

"What is it, Nan?" he asked.

"I—I—oh, Mr. Tetlow, won't you please let Bert off this time? He only did it because Danny said such things about me; said I was afraid of the ghost, and made all the boys call out that we had a ghost at our house. I—I—think, somehow, that I ought to be punished if he is."

There, it was out, and Nan felt the better for it. Her deep brown eyes looked squarely into the eyes of the principal.

In spite of himself Mr. Tetlow was compelled to smile. He knew something of how the Bobbsey twins were devoted to each other.

"So you think you ought to be punished," he said slowly.

"Yes, if Bert is, for you see, he did it mostly for me."

"You are a brave sister to come in his behalf, Nan. I shall not punish him very severely."

"Oh, thank you for saying that, Mr. Tetlow."

"It was very wrong for him to fight—"

"Yes, I told him that."

"But Danny Rugg did wrong to provoke him. I sincerely trust that both boys forgive each other for what was done. Now you can go."

With a lighter heart Nan left the office. She felt that Bert would not be expelled. And he was not. Instead, Mr. Tetlow made him stay in an hour after school each day that week and write on his slate the sentence, "Fighting is wrong," a hundred times. Danny was also kept in and was made to write the sentence just twice as many times. Then Mr. Tetlow made the two boys shake hands and promise to do better in the future.

The punishment was nothing to what Bert had expected, and he stayed in after school willingly. But Danny was very sulky and plotted all manner of evil things against the Bobbseys.

"He is a very bad boy," said Nan. "If I were you, Bert, I'd have nothing more to do with him."

"I don't intend to have anything to do with him," answered her twin brother. "But, Nan, what do you think he meant when he said he'd make trouble about Mr. Ringley's broken window? Do you imagine he'll tell Mr. Ringley I broke it?"

"How would he dare, when he broke it himself?" burst out Nan.

"I'm sure I don't know. But if he did, what do you suppose Mr. Ringley would do?"

"I'm sure I don't know," came helplessly from Nan. "You can't prove that Danny did it, can you?"

"No."

"It's too bad. I wish the window hadn't been broken."

"So do I," said Bert; and there the talk came to an end, for there seemed nothing more to say.

St. Valentine's Day

St. Valentine's Day was now close at hand, and all of the children of the neighborhood were saving their money with which to buy valentines.

"I know just the ones I am going to get," said Nan.

"I want some big red hearts," put in Freddie. "Just love hearts, I do!"

"I want the kind you can look into," came from Flossie. "Don't you know, the kind that fold up?"

Two days before St. Valentine's Day the children gathered around the sitting-room table and began to make valentines. They had paper of various colors and pictures cut from old magazines. They worked very hard, and some of the valentines thus manufactured were as good as many that could be bought.

"Oh, I saw just the valentine for Freddie," whispered Nan to Bert. "It had a fireman running to a fire on it."

There were a great many mysterious little packages brought into the house on the afternoon before St. Valentine's Day, and Mr. Bobbsey had to supply quite a few postage stamps.

"My, my, but the postman will have a lot to do to-morrow," said Mr. Bobbsey. "If this keeps on he'll want his wages increased, I am afraid."

The fun began early in the morning. On coming down to breakfast each of the children found a valentine under his or her plate. They were all very pretty.

"Where in the world did they come from?" cried Nan. "Oh, mamma, did you put them there?"

"No, Nan," said Mrs. Bobbsey.

"Then it must have been Dinah!" said Nan, and rushed into the kitchen. "Oh, Dinah, how good of you!"

"'Spect da is from St. Valentine," said the cook, smiling broadly.

"Oh, I know you!" said Nan.

"It's just lubby!" cried Freddie, breaking out into his baby talk. "Just lubby, Dinah! Such a big red heart, too!"

The postman came just before it was time to start for school. He brought six valentines, three for Flossie, two for Freddie and one for Bert.

"Oh, Nan, where is yours?" cried Bert.

"I—I guess he forgot me," said Nan rather soberly.

"Oh, he has made some mistake," said Bert and ran after the letter man. But it was of no use—all the mail for the Bobbseys had been delivered.

"Never mind, he'll come again this afternoon," said Mrs. Bobbsey, who saw how keenly Nan was disappointed.

On her desk in school Nan found two valentines from her schoolmates. One was very pretty, but the other was home-made and represented a girl running away from a figure labeled GHOST. Nan put this out of sight as soon as she saw it.

All that day valentines were being delivered in various ways. Freddie found one in his cap, and Bert one between the leaves of his geography. Flossie found one pinned to her cloak, and Nan received another in a pasteboard box labeled Breakfast Food. This last was made of paper roses and was very pretty.

The letter man came that afternoon just as they arrived home from school. This time he had three valentines for Nan and several for the others. Some were comical, but the most of them were beautiful and contained very tender verses. There was much guessing as to who had sent each.

"I have received just as many as I sent out," said Nan, counting them over.

"I sent out two more than I received," said Bert.

"Never mind, Bert; boys don't expect so many as girls," answered Nan.

"I'd like to know who sent that mean thing that was marked GHOST," went on her twin brother.

"It must have come from Danny Rugg," said Bert, and he was right. It had come from Danny, but Nan never let him know that she had received it, so his hoped-for fun over it was spoilt.

In the evening there was more fun than ever. All of the children went out and dropped valentines on the front piazzas of their friends' houses. As soon as a valentine was dropped the door bell would be given a sharp ring, and then everybody would run and hide and watch to see who came to the door.

When the Bobbsey children went home they saw somebody on their own front piazza. It was a boy and he was on his knees, placing something under the door mat.

"I really believe it is Danny Rugg!" cried Nan.

"Wait, I'll go and catch him," said Bert, and started forward.

But Danny saw him coming, and leaping over the side rail of the piazza, he ran to the back garden.

"Stop," called Bert. "I know you, Danny Rugg!"

"I ain't Danny Rugg!" shouted Danny in a rough voice. "I'm somebody else."

He continued to run and Bert made after him. At last Danny reached the back fence. There was a gate there, but this was kept locked by Sam, so that tramps might be kept out.

For the moment Danny did not know what to do. Then he caught hold of the top of the fence and tried to scramble over. But there was a sharp nail there and on this his jacket caught.

"I've got you now!" exclaimed Bert, and made a clutch for him. But there followed the sound of ripping cloth and Danny disappeared into the darkness, wearing a jacket that had a big hole torn in it.

"Was it really Danny?" questioned Nan, when Bert came back to the front piazza.

"Yes, and he tore his coat—I heard it rip."

"What do you think of that?"

Nan pointed to an object on the piazza, half under the door mat. There lay a dead rat, and around its neck was a string to which was attached a card reading, "Nan and Bert Bobbsey's Ghost."

"This is certainly awful," said Bert.

The noise on the piazza had brought Mrs. Bobbsey to the door. At the sight of the dead rat, which Freddie had picked up by the tail, she gave a slight scream.

"Oh, Freddie, leave it go!" she said.

"It won't hurt you, mamma," said the little boy. "The real is gone out of it."

"But—but—how did it get here?"

"Danny Rugg brought it," said Bert. "Look at the tag."

He cut the tag off with his pocket-knife and flung the rat into the garbage can. All went into the house, and Mrs. Bobbsey and her husband both read what Danny Rugg had written on the card.

"This is going too far," said Mr. Bobbsey. "I must speak to Mr. Rugg about this." And he did the very next day. As a result, and for having torn his jacket, Danny received the hardest thrashing he had got in a year. This made him more angry than ever against Bert, and also angry at the whole Bobbsey family. But he did not dare to do anything to hurt them at once, for fear of getting caught.

Winter was now going fast, and before long the signs of spring began to show on every hand.

Spring made Freddie think of a big kite that he had stored away, in the garret, and one Saturday he and Bert brought the kite forth and fixed the string and the tail.

"There is a good breeze blowing," said Bert. "Let us go and fly it on Roscoe's common."

"I want to see you fly the kite," said Flossie. "Can I go along?"

"Yes, come on," said Bert.

Flossie had been playing with the kitten and hated to leave it. So she went down to the common with Snoop in her arms.

"Don't let Snoop run away from you," said Bert. "He might not find his way back home."

The common was a large one with an old disused barn at one end. Freddie and Bert took the kite to one end and Freddie held it up while Bert prepared to let out the string and "run it up," as he called it.

Now, as it happened, the eyes of Snoop were fixed on the long tail of the kite, and when it went trailing over the ground Snoop leaped from Flossie's arms and made a dash for it. The kitten's claws caught fast in the tail, and in a moment more the kite went up into the air and Snoop with it.

"Oh, my kitten!" called out Freddie. "Snoop has gone up with the kite!"

The Rescue of Snoop, the Kitten

It was certainly something that nobody had been expecting, and as the kite went higher and higher, and Snoop with it, both Flossie and Freddie set up a loud cry of fear.

"Snoop will be killed!" exclaimed the little girl. "Oh, poor dear Snoop!" and she wrung her hands in despair.

"Let him down!" shrieked Freddie. "Oh, Bert, please let my dear kitten down, won't you?"

Bert did not hear, for he was running over the common just as hard as he could, in his endeavor to raise the kite. Up and up it still went, with poor Snoop dangling helplessly at the end of the swaying tail.

At last Bert ran past the old barn which I have already mentioned. Just as he did this he happened to look up at the kite.

"Hullo, what's on the tail?" he yelled. "Is that a cat?"

"It's Snoop!" called out Freddie, who was rushing after his big brother. "Oh, Bert, do let him down. If he falls, he'll be killed."

"Well, I never!" ejaculated Bert.

He stopped running and gradually the kite began to settle close to the top of the barn. Poor Snoop was swinging violently at the end of the ragged tail. The swinging brought the frightened creature closer still to the barn, and all of a sudden Snoop let go of the kite tail and landed on the shingles.

"Snoop is on the barn!" cried Bert, as the kite settled on the grass a few yards away.

"Oh, Snoop! Snoop! are you hurt?" cried Freddie, running back a distance, so that he might get a view of the barn top.

Evidently Snoop was not hurt. But he was still scared, for he stood on the edge of the roof, with his tail standing straight up.

"Meow! meow! meow!" he said plaintively.

"He is asking for somebody to take him down," said Freddie. "Aren't you, Snoop?"

"Meow!" answered the black kitten.

"Oh, dear me, what will you do now?" cried Flossie, as she came chasing up.

"Perhaps I can get to the roof from the inside," said Bert, and he darted quickly into the barn.

There were a rickety pair of stairs leading to the barn loft and these he mounted. In the loft all was dark and full of cobwebs. Here and there were small holes through the roof, through which the water came every time it rained.

"Snoop! Snoop!" he called, putting his mouth close to one of the holes.

The kitten turned around in surprise. He hardly knew from whence the voice came, but he evidently knew Bert was calling, for he soon came in that direction.

As the barn was an old one and not fit to use, Bert felt it would do no harm to knock a shingle or two from the roof. Looking around, he espied a stout stick of wood lying on the floor and with this he began an attack on the shingles and soon had two of them broken away.

"Come, Snoop!" he called, looking out of the hole. "Come here!"

But the sound of the blows had frightened the kitten, and Snoop had fled to the slope of the roof on the opposite side of the barn.

"Where is he?" called the boy, to the twins below.

"Gone to the other side," said Freddie. "Don't like the noise, I guess."

"Chase him over here," returned Bert.

Both Freddie and Flossie tried to do so. But Snoop would not budge, but stood on the very edge of the roof, as if meditating a spring to the ground.

"Don't jump, please don't jump, Snoop!" pleaded Flossie. "If you jump you'll surely break a leg, or maybe your back!"

Whether Snoop understood this or not, it would be hard to say. But he did not jump, only stayed where he was and meowed louder than ever.

"Can't you drive him over?" asked Bert, after a long wait.

"Won't come," said Freddie. "Wants to jump down, I guess."

Hearing this, Bert ran down to the lower floor and outside.

"Can't you get a ladder?" asked Flossie. "Perhaps Mr. Roscoe will lend you one."

Mr. Roscoe lived at the other end of the common. He was a very old and very quiet man, and the majority of the girls and boys in Lakeport were afraid of him. He lived all alone and was thought to be queer.

"I—I can see," said Bert hesitatingly.

He ran across the common to Mr. Roscoe's house and rapped on the door. Nobody came and he rapped again, and then a third time.

"Who's there?" asked a voice from within.

"Please, Mr. Roscoe, is that you?" asked Bert.

"Yes."

"Well, our kitten is on the top of your old barn and can't get down. Can you lend me a ladder to get him down with?"

"Kitten on my barn? How did he get there?" and now the old man opened the door slowly and cautiously. He was bent with age and had white hair and a long white beard.

"He went up with a kite," said Bert, and explained the case, to which the old man listened with interest.

"Well! well! well!" exclaimed Mr. Roscoe, in a high piping voice. "Going to take a sail through the air, was he? You'll have to build him a balloon, eh?"

"I think he had better stay on the ground after this."

"He must be a high-flyer of a cat," and the old man chuckled over his joke.

"Will you lend me a ladder?" went on Bert.

"Certainly, my lad. The ladder is in the cow-shed yonder. But you'll have to raise it yourself, or get somebody to raise it for you. My back is too old and stiff for such work."

"I'll try it alone first," answered the boy.

He soon had the long ladder out and was dragging it across the common. It was very heavy and he wondered who he could get to help him raise it. Just then Danny Rugg came along.

"What are you doing with old Roscoe's ladder?" he asked.

Bert was on the point of telling Danny it was none of his business, but he paused and reflected. He wanted no more quarrels with the big boy.

"I am going to get our cat down from the barn roof," he answered.

"Humph!"

"Do you want to help me raise the ladder, Danny?"

"Me? Not much! You can raise your own ladder."

"All right, I will, if you don't want to help me," said Bert, the blood rushing to his face.

"So that's your cat, is it?" cried Danny, looking toward the barn. "I wouldn't have such a black beast as that! We've got a real Maltese at our house."

"We like Snoop very much," answered Bert, and went on with his ladder.

Danny hunted for a stone, and watching his chance threw it at Snoop. It landed close to the kitten's side and made Snoop run to the other side of the barn roof.

"Stop that, Danny Rugg!" cried a voice from the other end of the common, and Nan appeared. She had just heard about the happening to Snoop and was hurrying to the spot to see if she could be of assistance.

"Oh, go on with your old cat!" sneered Danny, and shuffled off past Mr. Roscoe's house.

The old man had come out to see what Bert was going to do with the ladder, and now he came face to face with Danny Rugg.

"Well, is it possible!" murmured the old man to himself. "That boy must belong around here after all!"

When Bert reached the barn he found a dozen boys collected, and several volunteered to assist him in raising the long ladder. It was hard work, and once the ladder slipped, but in the end it rested against the barn roof and then Bert went up in a hurry.

"Come, Snoop!" he called, and the kitten came and perched himself on Bert's shoulder.

When Bert came down the ladder those standing around set up a cheer, and Freddie and Flossie clapped their hands in delight.

"Oh, I'm so glad you got him back!" said Freddie and hugged the kitten almost to death.

"What boy was that who threw the stone?" asked Mr. Roscoe of Nan, while Bert was returning the ladder to the cow-shed.

"That was Danny Rugg," answered Nan. "He is a bad boy."

"I know he is a bad boy," said Mr. Roscoe. "A very bad boy indeed." And then the old man hurried off without another word. What he said meant a good deal, as we shall soon see.

The Last of the Ghost—good-night

The rescue of the kitten was the main subject of conversation that evening in the Bobbsey household.

"I never dreamed he would go up with the kite," said Flossie. "After this we'll have to keep him in the house when Bert and Freddie do their kite-flying."

Bert had seen Danny Rugg throw the stone at the kitten and was very angry over it. He had also seen Danny talk to Nan.

"I think he's an awful boy," declared Nan. "And Mr. Roscoe thinks he is bad, too."

"He had better stop throwing things or he'll get himself into trouble before long," said Bert.

"It's queer Mr. Ringley never heard about the window," whispered his twin sister.

"So it is. But it may come out yet," replied the brother.

That evening the Bobbseys had their first strawberry shortcake of the season. It was a beautiful cake—one of Dinah's best—and the strawberries were large and luscious.

"Want another piece," said Freddie, smacking his lips. "It's so good, mamma!"

"Freddie, I think you have had enough," said Mrs. Bobbsey.

"Oh, mamma, just a little piece more!" pleaded Freddie, and received the piece, much to his satisfaction.

"Strawberries is beautiful," he declared. "I'm going to raise a whole lot on the farm this summer."

"Oh, mamma, are we going to Uncle Dan's farm this summer?" burst out Nan eagerly.

"Perhaps, Nan," was the reply. "I expect a letter very shortly."

"Meadow Brook is a dandy place," said Bert. "Such a fine swimming hole in the brook!"

"Oh, I love the flowers, and the chickens and cows!" said Flossie.

"I like the rides on the loads of hay," said Nan.

The children talked the subject over until it was time to go to bed. Their Uncle Dan and Aunt Sarah lived at Meadow Brook, and so did their cousin Harry, a boy a little older than Bert, and one who was full of fun and very good-natured in the bargain.

Bert went to bed with his head full of plans for the summer. What glorious times they could have after school closed if they went to their uncle's farm!

It was a full hour before Bert got to sleep. The room was quite bright, for the moon was shining in the corner window. The moon made him think of the ghost he had once seen and he gave a little shudder. He never wanted to see that ghost again.

Bert had been asleep less than an hour when he awoke with a start. He felt sure somebody had touched him on the foot. He opened his eyes at once and looked toward the end of his bed.

The ghost was standing there!

At first Bert could scarcely believe that he saw aright. But it was true and he promptly dove under the covers.

Then he thought of Danny Rugg's cry, "Afraid of a ghost!" and he felt that he ought to have more courage.

"I'm going to see what that is," he said to himself, and shoved back the covers once more.

The figure in white had moved toward the corner of the room. It made no noise and Bert wondered how it would turn next.

"Wonder what will happen if I grab it, or yell?" he asked himself.

With equal silence Bert crawled out of bed. Close at hand stood his base-ball bat, which he had used a few days before. It made a formidable club, and he took hold of it with a good deal of satisfaction.

"Want another piece of strawberry shortcake," came to his ears. "Please give me another piece of strawberry shortcake."

Bert could hardly believe his ears. It was the ghost that was speaking! It wanted strawberry shortcake!

"Freddie!" he almost shouted. "Freddie, is it you?"

The ghost did not answer, but turned towards the door leading into the hallway. Bert ran after the figure in white and caught it by the arm.

The ghost was really Freddie, and he was walking in his sleep, with his eyes tightly closed.

"Well, I declare!" murmured Bert. "Why didn't we think of this before?"

"Please let me have another piece of strawberry shortcake, mamma," pleaded the sleep-walker. "Just a tiny little piece."

Bert had heard that it was a bad thing to awaken a sleep-walker too suddenly, so he took Freddie's arm very gently and walked the little fellow back to his bedroom and placed him on his bed. Then he shook him very gently.

"Oh!" cried Freddie. "Oh! Wha—what do you want? Let me sleep! It isn't time to get up yet."

"Freddie, I want you to wake up," said Bert.

"Who is talking?" came from across the hallway, in Mr. Bobbsey's voice.

"I'm talking, papa," answered Bert. He ran to the doorway of his parents' bedchamber. "I've just found out who the ghost is," he continued.

"The ghost?" Mr. Bobbsey leaped up. "Where is it?"

"In bed now. It was Freddie, walking in his sleep. He was asking for another piece of strawberry shortcake."

By this time the whole household was wide awake.

"Oh, Freddie, was it really you?" cried Nan, going to the little fellow.

"Wasn't walking in my sleep," said Freddie. "Was dreaming 'bout shortcake, that's all. Want to go to sleep again," and he turned over on his pillow.

"Let him sleep," said Mrs. Bobbsey. "We'll have to consult the doctor about this. He will have to have something for his digestion and eat less before going to bed in the future." And the next day the doctor was called in and gave Freddie something which broke up the sleep-walking to a very large extent.

"I am glad you caught Freddie," said Nan, to her twin brother. "If you hadn't, I should always have believed that we had seen a ghost."

"Glad I don't walk in my sleep," said Flossie. "I might tumble downstairs and break my nose."

"I shall watch Freddie in the future," said Mrs. Bobbsey, and she did.

When Bert went to school the next day he met Danny Rugg and the tall boy glared at him very angrily.

"Think you are smart, don't you?" said Danny. "I'm not going to stand it, Bert Bobbsey."

"Oh, Bert, come along and don't speak to him," whispered Nan, who was with her twin brother.

"Went and saw Ringley, didn't you?" went on Danny, edging closer.

"Keep away, Danny Rugg," answered Bert. "I want nothing to do with you, and I haven't been to see Mr. Ringley."

"Yes, you did go and see him," insisted Danny. "Wasn't he to see my father last night?"

"Did Mr. Ringley come to see your father?" asked Bert curiously.

"Yes, he did. And my father—but never mind that now," broke off the tall boy. He had been on the point of saying that his father had given him a severe thrashing. "I'm going to fix you, Bert Bobbsey."

"Don't you dare to strike my brother, Danny Rugg!" put in Nan, stepping in between them.

How much further the quarrel might have gone, it is impossible to say, for just then Mr. Tetlow put in an appearance, and Danny sneaked off in great haste.

When the children came from school they learned that Mrs. Bobbsey had been down-town, buying some shoes for herself and Flossie.

"Mr. Ringley was telling me about his broken window," said she to her husband. "He found out that Danny Rugg broke it. Old Mr. Roscoe saw Danny do it. He didn't know Danny at the time, but he has found out since who Danny was."

"That Rugg boy is a bad one," answered Mr. Bobbsey. "I suppose Mr. Ringley made the Ruggs pay for the window."

"Oh, yes, and Mr. Rugg said he was going to correct Danny, too."

The children heard this talk, but said nothing at the time. But later Nan called Bert out into the garden.

"I see it all," she whispered to her twin brother. "That's why Mr. Roscoe asked me who Danny was, and that's why he said Danny was such a bad boy."

"I'm glad in one way that Danny has been found out," answered Bert, "for that clears me." And he was right, for he never heard of the broken window again.

The children were still waiting anxiously for a letter from their Uncle Dan or their Aunt Sarah. At last a letter came and they listened to it with great delight.

"Oh, what do you think?" cried Nan, dancing up to Bert. "We are to go to Meadow Brook as soon as vacation begins!"

"Good!" shouted Bert, throwing his cap into the air. "Won't we have the best times ever was!" And this proved to be a fact. What happened to the Bobbsey twins at Meadow Brook will be told in another book, which I shall call, "The Bobbsey Twins in the Country." The country is a lovely place, especially in the summer time, and all of my young readers can rest assured that the twins enjoyed themselves at Meadow Brook to the utmost.

"I'll be so glad to see Cousin Harry again," said Bert.

"And I'll be glad to see Aunt Sarah," piped in Freddie. "She makes such *beautiful* pies!"

"Think of the lovely big barn," put in Flossie. "It's just like a—a palace to play in on wet days!"

"Oh, Flossie, to compare a barn to a palace!" exclaimed Nan. "But it is a nice place after all," she added, after a moment's thought.

That evening, to celebrate the good news, the twins gave a little party to half a dozen of their most intimate friends. There were music and singing, and all sorts of games, and a magic-lantern exhibition by one of the boys. All enjoyed it greatly and voted the little party a great success.

"Good-night! Good-night!" said the young folks to each other, when the party broke up. And here let us say good-night, too, for my little story has reached its end.

THE END

Made in the USA
Coppell, TX
12 September 2021

62226649R10062